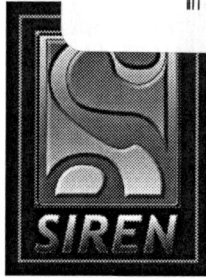

Made for Each Other

When librarian Lesley Farmer meets builder Charlene McKinley, it's hot at first sight. Pheromones flood common sense despite the fact that each is so obviously not the other's type. He prefers women who are sophisticated, genteel, and ultra-feminine. She prefers men who are buff and don't wear bowties. But when hormones take over, the two ravished and bemused opposites are left to see what they can build together.

Through a series of assumptions and misconceptions, it seems as if the unlikely pair will never get together. Maybe all they really shared was a one-night stand after all. Yet neither can stop thinking about the other. When fate puts them together one more time, they say to hell with dating and head straight to bed.

But can home-and-hearth-seeking Lesley convince commitment-shy Charlie that building a life together is inevitable because they are made for each other?

Erotic Romantic Comedy

REVIEWS for Morgan Ashbury's
MADE FOR EACH OTHER

5 HEARTS: "What an addictive story! To say that Lesley Farmer and Charlie McKinley were polar opposites would be like comparing the Grand Canyon to a hole! Dr. Lesley Farmer was a university Director of Library Services; Charlie McKinley was a building contractor with four brothers; she was the only one without a formal higher education, but the family knew she was actually the smartest member. The couple met early one morning when Lesley needed someone to come to his aid after a huge tree which was formerly in his backyard ended up in his upstairs bedroom. Incredibly, that was only part of their problem; their sexual attraction to each other was indescribable and such a shock to them! Ms. Morgan Ashbury has written a phenomenal story with a unique plot which, I predict, will be an award winner. Her characters are strong: both Lesley and Charlie have strong foundational relationships with others; it is just commitment that is hard to accept! Ms. Ashbury has an extensive ability to bring their likenesses to light without rambling. There is so much substance in this novel that it would be very easy to bog down in wordiness; it would be simple to lose readers. However, after reading this book, I am delighted that she could share so much information in this superb manner. Seldom have I read a book I enjoyed more; that this is Ms. Ashbury's first book is amazing. I highly recommend this book to all who are interested in a beautiful love story which has a light comedic appeal!" —**Brenda Talley,** *The Romance Studio*

4 CUPS: "*Made for Each Other* is a powerhouse read. It was fun watching the mismatch duo tackle their feelings for the other. I love it when two people suddenly interact instantly, and their chemistry burns the pages. Charlie and Lesley are dynamite individuals with great personalities. Ms. Ashbury details a story that captivates and wins the heart of this reader. The way she instilled the desire for commitment into the storyline made the story even more enjoyable as the reader feels a part of the couple's relationship. This romantic story is an absolute delight." —**Cherokee,** *Coffee Time Romance*

"What do a builder and a librarian have in common? Seemingly nothing, but Charlene McKinley and Lesley Farmer can't help but find each other simply irresistible in Morgan Asbury's *Made For Each Other*. Charlene and Lesley are unique, believable characters who are a treat to read. Their enjoyable, seductive story immediately draws the reader in. The secondary characters - Charlie and Lesley's best friends, family, and coworkers are also well drawn and not just background players. But it's Charlie and Lesley's passionate relationship with all of its ups and downs that is captivating. Ashbury is fabulous at telling a romantic, spicy story with easy-to-love characters. Look for more from this talented debut writer in the future." —**Amy Mendenhall,** *NewsandSentinel.com*

DEDICATION

I'm a much better writer today than I was four years ago because an author named Kelley Armstrong started the Online Writers' Group. So, to Kelley and my fellow OWG members Raina, Ian, Chris, and John, and Amy, one of my two critique partners, whose assistance with this story was invaluable.

To my family, who has put up with having an 'artiste' in their midst. And especially for David, who never doubted this moment would come. And for Anthony, who didn't get to see it.

Morgan Ashbury
www.MorganAshbury.com

MADE FOR EACH OTHER

Morgan Ashbury

To Helen
with love
and great thanks
that I found you!

Love Morgan Ashbury

EROTIC ROMANCE

Siren Publishing, Inc.
www.SirenPublishing.com

A SIREN PUBLISHING BOOK
IMPRINT: Erotic Romance

MADE FOR EACH OTHER
Copyright © 2007 by Morgan Ashbury
ISBN-10: 1-933563-02-8
ISBN-13: 978-1-933563-02-2

First Printing, April 2007

Cover design by Jinger Heaston
All cover art and logo copyright © 2007 by Siren Publishing, Inc.

Printed in the U.S.A.

PUBLISHER
Siren Publishing, Inc.
www.SirenPublishing.com

MADE FOR EACH OTHER

MORGAN ASHBURY

Chapter 1

He was hard, and it was all her fault.

The way Lesley Farmer saw it, he had two immediate problems. The first, and most urgent, hung six feet above his head in the master bedroom. Sporting dark brown limbs and lush green leaves, the Manitoba Maple had been upright and stalwart, shading his back yard, up until about two hours ago. Now it seemed intent on making a place for itself indoors. The second problem, less obvious, he hoped, hung between his legs. It was the fastest and strongest erection he'd ever sprouted and would appear to have been inspired solely by the presence of the woman standing next to him.

"That is one big piece of wood," contractor Charlie McKinley said.

Lesley kept his eyes focused on the 'break and enter' tree, bit back the 'thank-you' that rolled from his throat to his tongue, and murmured his agreement. He was trying to figure out just what it was about this woman that set his sap to rising. She was definitely not his usual type. He liked petite, dainty women. 'Dainty' didn't suit Ms. McKinley. She almost matched his six one height, and her blond hair was cut in a sleek, face-framing cap. Form fitting jeans and tee left no doubt of her femininity, though. She *was* very easy on the eyes, and there was no mistaking the affect she was having on his body. He just hoped that her attention would remain on the intrusive limb above their heads, and that she would not discover the one in his pants.

"From my experience," she continued, "I can tell you that it's going to require expert handling."

"You're not qualified to take care of it yourself, then?"

"I'd need a crane to lift that sucker."

She said sucker. Lesley had to use every ounce of his willpower to pull his mind away from sex and focus it on the situation at hand. He figured that if he didn't, his mouth was going to get him into deep, serious trouble. So he gave the brown and green intruder one more detailed study, then boldly turned to face Ms. McKinley. His focus was entirely on her, his question direct, spoken as if he *didn't* have a raging hard-on between his legs.

"Do you know anyone who has the expertise to handle it?"

"Yes, I know a guy who runs a tree service. His rates are the best in town. But the roof and interior ceiling repair, once the tree's out, are things that I can do."

Lesley nodded briskly, once, then turned his attention back to the tree. He'd caught the slight flicker of her eyes away from his face and knew that she'd seen his condition. *Well, this is probably the most embarrassing moment of my life to date.* He was a man. He was tough. He could take it…he hoped.

From his peripheral vision, he watched as Ms. McKinley brought her glazed eyes back into focus, licked her lips, swallowed, then fastened her attention overhead on the tree. *Maybe not so embarrassing if she liked what she saw.*

"I won't be able to begin an estimate on the repairs until that woody…I mean tree…is out of that hole…off the roof."

He swallowed his laughter as he realized he wasn't the only one affected by raging hormones. That was a relief. Even as he considered the situation, his own eyes wandered, and caught the beading of her nipples, just discernable under the covering of her t-shirt. It occurred to him then that they had both been silent for a long time, staring at that damn tree as if it was the most fascinating sight either of them had ever seen. He was trying to figure out what to do next when the sound of the grandfather clock in the living room announcing the half hour snapped Lesley back to reality. *Hell, he was going to be late.*

"If you'd be so kind as to arrange for this tree to be removed, Ms. McKinley, I'd appreciate it. I'd also like an estimate on the repair. I don't know if my insurance company will want additional quotes or not. I'll have to get back to you on that."

"Some do, some don't," she replied as she opened her clipboard. "If you'll just give me a few moments and answer a couple of routine questions, I'll fill out a work order for you to sign, sir."

Her snooty tone caught him off guard. It certainly wasn't *his* fault that they were both in this strange erogenous zone. *Screw it, two can play that game.* "My neighbor, Mrs. Crosby, will be over in a moment and will lock up after you're done, Ms. McKinley. I have to get to the university library. Here's my number, you can let me know when that estimate is ready."

He held out the business card and raised one eyebrow, daring her to take it. Her frown told him he'd scored a bulls-eye with his response.

"You have to go to the library? *Now*?"

"Since I'm the Director of Library Services, I'd better."

"I appreciate the business, Mr. Farmer. I'll see if I can get Jake over immediately to get this tree out. Then I'll cover the hole with a tarp. The forecast isn't calling for rain, but it is spring in southern Ontario. You just never know."

"Thank you, Ms. McKinley." Considering her for a moment, he gave in to his inner imp. "I wouldn't want to get…wet in my bed."

"Well, if I have anything to say about it, Mr. Farmer, you'll stay as dry and safe as a kitten."

* * * *

Charlie heaved a huge sigh of relief once Lesley Farmer drove off. Never in her entire life had she encountered a situation like this, and it wasn't the tree she was thinking about. The moment Lesley Farmer had opened his door, she'd been hit by the most bizarre reaction. She was instantly randy, ready, and raring to go.

At least her body was. It was rarely necessary for Charlie to grab the reins of her libido and yell "whoa!" Today, however, she'd clutched them in both hands with her heels dug in for extra measure. *Measure*. Yeah, that was part of the problem. Well, part two of the entire problem. Not only was she hornier than she'd ever been, but, judging by the shape she'd eyeballed in the front of his pants, so was Lesley Farmer.

Being instantly turned on was a condition that, with quick thinking and a sincere expression, she could explain away using the wonderful female catchall, 'hormones.' That Lesley Farmer could turn her on had no explanation whatsoever. Sure, he was tall and good-looking. He had a build that told her he likely worked out on a regular basis, but he wasn't as buff as her usual type. And while she had often felt mild attraction when first meeting a man, she had never been so instantly hot and wet.

He was *so* not her type. He worked in the university library. What could they possibly have in common?

The words *raging hormones* immediately came to mind and she ruthlessly banished them. Unfortunately, while her attention was fixed on getting rid of inappropriate words, inappropriate images bloomed.

Man, that guy was hung. His was the largest erection she had ever seen. Not that she'd actually seen it. In the flesh, that is. What a damn shame that she likely never would.

Her attention was drawn back to Mrs. Crosby.

"Oh my," the elderly woman commented when she walked into the master bedroom. "What a blessing that this didn't happen when Edith lived here. Why, the shock would have killed her!"

Since Edith Farmer had passed away three months before, Charlie thought it prudent to refrain from comment.

"But I just don't understand," Mrs. Crosby continued. "There wasn't a storm, or even a strong wind this morning. Yet I did hear it fall, oh yes, I did. I ran to my back door and looked out, and then I thought to myself, 'Sarah, thank goodness that Edith didn't live to see this!' Oh, my, that really wasn't a nice thought, was it? But I just don't understand!"

Charlie blinked as her brain raced to keep up, putting the elderly woman's words in logical order. Deciding to keep her cheekier comments to herself, she instead addressed the matter of the fallen tree.

"Manitoba Maples are like the weeds of the tree family. At least, that's what my gramps used to say. Sometimes they rot from the inside out. Gramps had one on his property and it fell too, on a day much like this, with no warning whatsoever."

"When that tree man comes, perhaps I better ask him about that old tree in *my* backyard. I think it's one of those western trees, too. You know, I heard that the people out west resented us Ontarians, but I *never* imagined they would send us a sabotaging tree!"

Charlie opened her mouth and then closed it again. Mrs. Crosby reminded her of her Great Aunt Katie. Aunt Katie was a sweet little thing, but not terribly concerned about facts.

"I'll see to it that Jake makes a point of speaking with you," Charlie responded, and couldn't help but return the wide grin the elderly woman gave her.

* * * *

"Sorry I'm late," Lesley announced as he entered the conference room. He was, in fact, five minutes late for the staff meeting. Lesley was never late for meetings.

"Not a problem, sir." Melissa Champlain, his executive assistant, was able to speak with respect and preen like a courtesan at the same time. It was an awesome thing to witness when one was interviewing for the position of Director of Library Services. It was another thing entirely when one *was* the director, coping with the young woman's repeated flirtations on a daily basis.

There were two things about Melissa's campaign that doomed it to failure right from the start. The first, and inviolable, was that as a member of his staff she was, according to his personal code of ethics, completely off limits. The second, and in light of the day's events, most troubling, was that she actually left him cold. Which shouldn't be the case, because Melissa was *just* the sort of woman that Lesley had always considered his type. She was petite, feminine and stacked.

"Melissa, I'm expecting calls this morning from a contractor, as well as my insurance agent. Please put them through immediately."

"Certainly sir. I hope nothing is wrong."

Lesley caught the snickers of a couple of his staff members, but ignored them. "Nothing terribly bad. Had a tree collapse, landing on the roof of my house this morning. Heck of an alarm clock, if you ask me."

"Oh my goodness! You weren't hurt?"

This time the snickering was quieter, and Lesley wanted to say, *"Yes, as you can see from the bandages covering me, I suffered many contusions and abrasions."* Instead, he just shook his head in the negative, took in the waiting, expectant, and amused faces of the dozen other people gathered around the table, and said, "Let's begin, shall we?"

The meeting progressed as any Monday morning meeting progressed. By the time it was over, Lesley had developed one hell of a headache that seemed to be fuelled by Melissa's sickly sweet perfume.

Leaving his staff to chat among themselves, he made good his escape, heading for the sanctity of his office. Changing locations eased the pounding in his skull, but brought into sharper focus the images that had been distracting him since he left his house earlier. There, center stage, as she had been throughout his morning meeting, in living color and gloriously naked, was Charlie McKinley. Even as his intellect tried to reaffirm that the attractive contractor was *not* his type, his body was readying itself for action.

Lesley shook his head in denial. He was a man who was used to being in control of himself, as well as most situations. It was just a matter of defining the intention and focusing the will.

There was certainly no question of which of the two of his heads governed *him*.

Chapter 2

She couldn't stop thinking about his cock.

The tree had been reduced to manageable pieces that were resting in the back of a truck. Charlie had taken the measurements and inspected the damage. Sometimes, when dealing with a hole in a roof, she had crafted a temporary patch that would, in all likelihood, last for months. She did not, however, get the sense that Lesley Farmer was the sort of man who would put off doing what needed to be done. If his insurer only required one estimate, she'd bet that he would see to it that the work was begun before the week was out.

Charlie shook her head. Why should she be getting warm, gooey feelings in her belly from thinking about a man who was not her type? Well, okay, there was the obvious. *Man, had it been obvious. I didn't even know a man could be hung that well.* The thought caused Charlie to miss the step up to her truck, and she banged her knee on the running board.

"*Shit.* I have got to get that man's penis out of my thoughts," she muttered, grateful no one could hear her. How she was going to do that, she didn't have a clue. Her mind had never grappled with the problem before.

She headed the truck for home. In times past, just walking through the front door would help her settle whatever was troubling her. There'd be the smell of cookies or soup, and Mom. But Charlie's parents were currently on their 'retirement tour.' They had purchased a mobile home the year before and set off to discover the continent. They were planning to swing into town sometime in August. That was still several months away, and Charlie wasn't the least bit ashamed to say that she was really looking forward to seeing them. She missed her parents terribly.

She pulled her truck into the second driveway, the one that angled down and ended not far from the basement entrance to the house. Tossing her clipboard onto her paper-strewn desk, she ran a hand through her hair and took in the general clutter that surrounded her. Home gym to the left, home office to the right, with no partition to separate the two. Not a problem so far, she thought as she headed upstairs. It would be nice, though, to have her own place, not just for her business but for herself.

She wended her way through the kitchen to the stairs that led to the second level where her bedroom was. She shut the bedroom door behind her and just sprawled on the bed for a moment as her thoughts continued to circle.

Overall, it wasn't bad living with her three bachelor brothers, especially since they all finally understood that she wasn't a servant to clean up after them. Also, they were all adults. If anyone wanted an overnight guest, the others simply looked the other way.

That was to say, *Charlie* looked the other way. She had never been brave enough to bring a man home for an overnight romp in her bed and cereal the next morning at the family dining table, so she really couldn't say how her brothers would react to such an event.

Charlie wasn't celibate because of principle. It had just been a long time since she had been in a relationship. She had definite standards, and didn't believe in casual sex. She liked sex, liked everything about it, but there had to be more than just the physical for her. That didn't necessarily mean love. She had never been in love, but there had to be mutual knowledge, respect, and affection.

She sat up and rubbed her hands over her face. *There she was thinking about sex again.* A quick check of her watch showed her that it was just two-thirty. No one else was home, nor would they be for a few hours yet. She had promised Mr. Farmer an estimate today, and she'd get to it. But first, she thought the kindest thing she could do for herself was to have a shower and take care of this lingering arousal. Maybe *then* she could get her mind off big cocks and back onto business, where it belonged.

* * * *

"Dr. Farmer, I can't tell you what a joy it is, for myself and the rest of the *Friends of the Library*, to have such a learned man as yourself at the helm of our University Library."

Then don't. "That's very kind of you to say, Mrs. Hamilton. I'll do my best not to disappoint."

With an ingratiating smile in place, Lesley brought his thoughts under control. Mrs. Hamilton was a patron of the library and it behooved him to pay attention and be nice. Images of naked contractors and pithy mental wisecracks had no place here.

You shouldn't even be here eating wilted salad with this old biddy. You should be getting it on with Charlie.

Lesley fought to push the wildly inappropriate thoughts away. He did not 'get it on' with women. He did, from time to time, become involved in monogamous relationships. While he'd never been in love, he wanted to be. He didn't treat women or his relationships with them in a cavalier manner. He considered himself a good lover, one with tender sensibilities who always made sure that his partner came first. And what the *hell* was he doing thinking of sex while he was seated at a restaurant table across from Mrs. Hamilton?

When the lady in question began to bat her eyes at him coquettishly, Lesley realized that it was time to leave. Using every bit of charm at his disposal, he ended the luncheon, determined that Mrs. Hamilton's breathily whispered, "another day, perhaps," never came to pass.

Lesley wasted no time getting to his car and putting the restaurant behind him. His gaze flicked to the dash clock. It was just after three, and he'd gotten very little accomplished today. A part of him wanted to just say to hell with it, and head home for a long, hot shower and a cold beer or two. The other part of him, the over-achieving-anal-librarian part, was screaming at him to return to the office and get back to work.

The secret to success, Lesley reasoned as he reached forward and pushed a button on his cell phone, was compromise.

"Dr. Farmer's office."

"Melissa, it's Dr. Farmer. Have there been any messages?"

"Yes, sir. A Mr. Garibaldi called, and so did someone named Charlie. He had a very funny sounding voice, sir. And he referred to you as *Mister* Farmer. Of course, I immediately corrected him."

"And the messages?" Lesley felt his patience slipping and shook his head. He really had to sit down soon and have a serious chat with his inner imp. Melissa Champlain was a woman with a very high I.Q. *She was not a ditz.*

"Well, Mr. Garibaldi didn't leave a message, he just left his number."

"I have it. And Charlie? What did she say?"

"She? Well, no wonder his voice sounded funny. He was a she! You know, she obviously doesn't have any respect for titles at all. If she had just called herself Ms. ...ah...McKinley, why then I would have known that she was a she and not a he."

"Melissa?"

"Sorry, sir. She said that the tree is gone, the hole covered, and the quote ready."

"Thanks. Anything else?"

"No, sir."

"All right, then. I won't be back this afternoon. You can call it a day, as well. I'll see you tomorrow."

He quickly dialed Marc Garibaldi, his insurance agent. The man had swung by the house, had a look at the damage, and taken the requisite pictures. Marc confirmed that there was no need to get competing quotes for the necessary repairs. *Good.* That meant he could give Charlie the go-ahead. His roof and ceiling would, hopefully, be repaired in short order and life could get back to normal. He tossed the headset for his cell phone onto the passenger seat. Not in the mood to receive any more calls, he also turned off the device. Reaching into his inside jacket pocket, he pulled out the copy of the work order Charlie McKinley had given him that morning. The form had not only her name, but her address as well. He wasn't as familiar with some parts of the city as he was with others, but he had a pretty good idea where Waverly Crescent was located. On the other side of town, it would take nearly a half hour to get there.

He mentally revised his immediate 'to do' schedule: Collect quote, authorize work, go home, shower, beer, and if the gods were smiling, there would be something worth watching on television.

* * * *

Water—warm, wet and wonderful—kissed her naked flesh in rhythmic, pulsing waves. Charlie relaxed her shoulders, arching her neck so that the tiny streams caressed her nipples. Eyes closed, she reached one hand out to cup body wash from the tube suspended by a rope from the showerhead. Slowly turning so that the heated water could massage her back, Charlie put her hands together, then brought them to her breasts.

Fragrant satin, the gel stimulated her as hands smoothed and cupped, fingers tweaking and pulling at her nipples. Behind her closed eyes, she surrendered to the images that had hovered all day. In her fantasy, a naked Lesley Farmer became her love slave. It was his hands that cupped the globes of her breasts, teasing the sensitive undersides, pinching and pulling.

Moaning with the pure pleasure the stroking gave her, one hand drifted slowly down and over her belly, caressing and combing through short blond hair. A soft hiss escaped her lips as soapy fingers sailed gently over her mound. *He would know just how to touch me,* she thought as fingers found and flicked her clitoris. The small button swelled almost instantly in response to the stimulation, and Charlie nearly cried out with the sharp sensation. Her palm slid over clit and slit, back and forth, spreading foam and fantasy. A deep aching emptiness gnawed at the pit of her belly, an emptiness that was hunger incarnate, female hunger for cock. Faster and faster her hand rubbed as her body built wave upon wave of arousal. Desperation for fulfillment seized her, and mindlessly she plunged first one then two fingers inside herself. Grinding her pussy against her hand she shouted, the rapture so sharp and intense she nearly fell to her knees. Wringing every last drop from the orgasm that she could, Charlie rested one shoulder against the tiled wall of the shower stall. A smile teased the corner of her mouth. That, she thought as she slowly straightened and turned her still throbbing body into the pulsing spray, was much better.

A few minutes later she was dressed and at her desk in the basement. She was more relaxed than she'd been in ages, she mused. It had been a long time since she'd had an orgasm in the middle of the afternoon. Hell, it had been a long time since she'd had one, period. She felt her face slide into a lazy smile. That was something she'd have to do for herself more often. She was a young, healthy woman who was currently unattached. Being unattached might limit the form of personal pleasure, but there was no reason not to see to her own needs from time to time. It could even be considered healthy, since the exercise should keep her from doing something really bizarre. *Like jumping Lesley Farmer.*

Shaking her head to dislodge the damn man from her thoughts, she put the day's events into perspective. Being a healthy young woman who had gone without sex for so long was the major reason, she believed, for that morning's hormonal attack. It had to be the reason, she asserted. She liked her men brawny and buff, the active type, but she also liked for them to be multi-faceted. You couldn't have sex all the time. There had better be something of substance in the relationship besides physical attraction. For Charlie that meant discussion, time spent in mutual recreation, and sharing similar tastes in music and food.

She couldn't imagine that she had anything in common with a librarian at all.

Well, you have one thing in common right now, and that's his roof. Before showering, she had called the number he'd given her to advise that the estimate on the roof repair was ready. *Or would be*, she mentally amended, *by the time he got there*. She'd resisted the urge to tell off the pissy woman at the other end of the phone who informed her *Doctor* Farmer would be given her message.

Charlie had the figures in her head and in her computer. All that was needed was to get busy and type up a quote. She had no idea how long the workday was for a Director of Library Services. Lesley Farmer seemed like the anal type, the sort of man who would stay at his desk–checking books or whatever it was he did–and likely wouldn't leave until six or six-thirty. That left her more than enough time to have the quote written, printed, and ready for pick up. It was also more than enough time to exorcise that man from her thoughts. With a sharp nod, she turned to her computer, opened all the documents she would need, logged onto the Internet, and got to work.

Half an hour later, the sound of a car in the drive had Charlie raising her head, frown in place. It was barely three-thirty. None of her brothers were due home until at least five. She wondered if she should get up and investigate. At just that moment, her printer began to spit out the last page of the quotation for the Farmer job. That was how she began to think of the work, and the man. The move had been a purely defensive one on her part. She shouldn't have been getting a nice little hum in her blood just thinking about him. She'd found the reason for the excitement of that morning, and had taken a hands-on approach to correcting it, as it were.

She caught the page as soon as the machine released it and stapled it to the previous one. She neatly added a cover letter to the quote and crisply folded the packet of pages in thirds. Inserting the whole shebang into an envelope, she asserted that she was *not* a coward to leave this package with whichever brother had just arrived home while she went…somewhere else. Then movement at the door caught her attention and her conviction faltered.

Chapter 3

He's wearing a tweed jacket and a bowtie and I am toast. How could she ever have guessed that seeing the man dressed in such staid clothing would turn her on like this? She swallowed hard and couldn't take her gaze away from his as he opened the screen door and came inside.

"You have something for me?"

The rasp of his voice sent shivers up and down her spine. Her eyes flicked to the front of his trousers, then back up again, and heat washed through her.

"I do?" Charlie was having trouble concentrating. She wondered how he knew what she wanted to give him. His condition was right out there, but there was no way he could see through her Capris to know...*he meant the quote.* Didn't he? She picked up the envelope that had slipped onto her desk from nerveless fingers. She noted that it was shaking in her hand and wondered why that was. Her nipples tightened painfully. She saw that Lesley had his gaze fastened on her hand as well. She would have thought, all things considered, that his line of sight would have been drawn higher by a few degrees. But it seemed as if he was working very hard to keep his eyes off her chest. That should have been calming. It shouldn't have been erotic and arousing, but it was.

"Do you have any idea what the hell is going on between us?" Lesley asked, his voice harsh, his breathing shallow.

"No. No idea. This has never happened to me before." Charlie dropped the envelope again and took two steps out to the side, away from her desk.

"Not to me, either. We're both mature, rational adults." Lesley took one step closer to her, a step that was forward and a little left of where he'd been standing.

"Right. Just because we're aware of a little chemistry," *Make that a bubbling cauldron of caustic chemicals,* she thought. Her lips were dry and she moistened them with her tongue.

"Doesn't mean we have to act on it," Lesley said.

She watched as he took one last step forward. She moved too, until mere inches separated them.

"Of course not. We're certainly in control of our own actions."

"Certainly."

Who took that last step Charlie couldn't say. The reality was that her body fused to his in a grasping embrace, her lips and tongue devouring his in a kiss that was hot, wild, and totally carnal. Moans and groans and gasps were interspersed with the action of her shirt being grabbed, removed, and dropped. Charlie shuddered and sighed. Her own hands stilled when her naked breasts were cupped in shaking male hands. *Ah, much better than my fantasy*, she thought. She melted as his deft fingers stroked and plucked and her nipples responded as if this was the touch they'd craved forever. Then, with renewed vigor, she continued the adventure of opening his shirt.

His chest was dusted with brown hair her hands were drawn to explore. Her lips slid into a Cheshire-cat grin as he cursed softly, his concentration broken. With definite devilry on her mind, she set her mouth on him, licking, nipping, and sucking.

"Minx. Give me your mouth," he whispered.

She fused her mouth on his again. Surprisingly strong arms lifted her up. She wrapped her arms around him and their lips locked, their tongues tasted and delved. One hand peeled the Capris from her body. There was no thought of resistance on her part, only of completion. She was being carried and she didn't care where. She heard the drag of a zipper, knew she was being lowered and wrapped her legs around his waist. The leather of the weightlifting bench was under her. He pulled her closer and still her mouth clung to his.

"Let me, baby, please let me," he whispered against her lips.

Reason fled, and all she cared about, all she *wanted*, was to feel this man, hot and hard, deep inside her. She breathed her agreement then shivered as the hot flesh of his cock nudged aside the crotch of her panties. In response to that heat, to the plea, her hips undulated forward.

"Shit. Fuck. Damn. Condom," he gasped.

"On the pill. I'm clean. *Please!*"

"Okay. Me, too. But still," one hand left her back and she felt him maneuvering. She caught sight of a wallet, then heard the crinkle of plastic.

"Don't leave home without it," he quipped between clenched teeth as he deftly rolled the protection on.

"Better than a credit card," she replied, torn between twin urges to laugh and scream.

Then she sighed as with one bold stroke he was buried in her to the hilt.

It didn't matter that they were sitting facing each other straddling an exercise bench. Only the contact between them mattered. Forehead to forehead, eyes locked, they rocked together and apart as the primal rhythm seized them both.

"Yeah, like that, deeper." Charlie's cries were in tune with the driving of his flesh into hers. Nothing was important except that she get as much of this magnificent thrusting as she could. His penis was big and she was stretched more than she'd ever been stretched before, but there was no discomfort, only a keen craving for more and still more.

"You're so hot and wet and tight around me."

His words enflamed her. Charlie whimpered, as she couldn't seem to get close enough to him. The rub of his trousers on her sensitive flesh, just below where they were joined was both an irritant and a stimulant. She was nearly overcome with the urge to lie back and surrender completely. When she moaned again, she felt his fingers seeking, and finding, her clitoris.

Charlie cried out as she came, her mouth eagerly fastening on Lesley's, feeling as if he was intent on devouring the sound. Then she felt the hot cock inside her begin to shudder as he came, and she knew they were devouring each other.

"My God," his words tickled the damp hair just brushing her shoulder, and she had to agree with the sentiment. But she struggled to tell him more.

"I've never..." She couldn't finish the sentence, and wasn't sure if she wanted to say she'd never had such a delicious, consuming orgasm, or that she'd never before become so intimate with someone she barely knew. In the next instant her heart melted as Lesley cupped her face and looked deeply into her eyes.

"I know. I do, Charlie. Me, neither."

* * * *

Before either of them could feel awkward, Lesley felt the ripple of Charlie's inner muscles around his shaft. He swore when his cock responded with renewed erection, and knew from her gasp that her arousal had spiked, too.

"This time," Lesley promised as he lifted her off the bench and brought her to the floor on an exercise mat, "this time, I'm going to fuck you deeper and longer."

He bore her to the floor without leaving her. And then he moving inside her again, hot and fast and deep.

He felt her legs wrap around him. When his mouth fastened on hers, when his hand reached up to fondle and squeeze her breast, he inwardly reveled as she surrendered completely.

"Yes," Lesley hissed, the male of the species recognizing the moment. "Yes, sweetheart, that's it, take everything I'm giving you.

Mine." He grunted as he thrust faster and faster, a part of him shocked that he could be so primitive, so rough. Yet even through the shock he couldn't wrest control from his body, couldn't exercise the governance of his mind. He should have felt guilty, was certain that he would, at some point soon. The sensation of female hands nearly clawing his back and strong female legs clamped around him as feminine hips pumped hard against him, however, quieted all sense of guilt.

"Come for me, Charlie. I want to feel you come on my cock again." Lesley's blood ignited into a fine fire as his hips plunged harder and faster. He'd never been gripped by such an obsession before. The deeper and faster he took, the more she gave and the more he needed. This was more than simple fucking. This was all-consuming, all-powerful. This was *mating*. And then he felt it along the length of his shaft, that strong wet rippling that told him her orgasm was bathing him with her essence. He held on for as long as he could, the pleasure so intense it nearly burned him, and then he was hurtling headlong into the fire, his ejaculation a fierce and awesome rapture.

For a long moment, the only sound was their labored breathing. Lesley was aware, vaguely, that he was letting his full weight rest on the woman beneath him. Yet he had no sense that he was crushing her, as her hands were gently stroking his damp back. His face was tucked into the hollow between her shoulder and her head, and with each breath, he inhaled her.

At last, he felt a return of some strength, and raised himself up on his arms. He looked into Charlie's eyes for a long, serious moment. He appreciated that she returned his solemn regard without flinching.

"This really wasn't what I planned to do when I got here," he said at last. "I think we'd better talk."

* * * *

She wanted to pretend it hadn't happened. Barring that, she wanted some time and space to pull herself together. She wasn't a coward though, and those actions would be cowardly. The echo of Lesley's confession was wringing in her ears, and it was a sentiment she shared. *She* hadn't planned to fuck the man, either.

She felt vulnerable, and that uncomfortable feeling was caused by more than just the nakedness of her body. Despite that, she looked him in the eyes and answered him.

"Yeah, you're right. We need to talk." Charlie exhaled heavily, and took the offer of a helping hand to get up from the floor. "I live with three of my brothers. Why don't we get dressed and...go for coffee somewhere?"

"Good idea. Go ahead and freshen yourself up. I'll wait here for you."

Charlie breathed a sigh of relief. He was allowing her a tactical withdrawal, a few moments of personal time to clean up, regroup. She scooped up her clothes and all but ran up the stairs. After spending a few necessary minutes in the bathroom, she headed for her bedroom. Her shirt and pants were in her hand, but for one moment she considered changing into jeans and a turtle neck sweater. And if she marched downstairs covered from head to foot, he'd probably laugh his head off at her. She wouldn't be able to blame him either. In the end, she grabbed a fresh pair of panties and a bra, but put her shirt and Capris back on. It was easy, and very tempting, to try and forget that she had just had hot sex—twice—in the basement with a man she'd only met that very day. It was tempting, but it wouldn't be honest. She might not know much about Lesley Farmer, librarian, but she did know this: whatever had just happened downstairs, whatever was happening between the two of them, he was as flummoxed by it and as unprepared for it as she was.

They had shared the dance, she thought as she faced herself squarely in the mirror. It was time, she supposed, to pay for the tune.

* * * *

Lesley fastened his pants and tried to catch his reflection in the chrome of the exercise equipment. He was grateful that the image reflected back wasn't very clear or detailed. He could see enough to know he was reasonably put together, but not well enough to read the expression on his face.

What in holy hell have I just done? He speared both hands through his hair in a gesture of bafflement. A flash of something caught his eye, and he turned his head slightly. There, dangling from Charlie's computer monitor, was his tie. For some reason the sight of the accessory caused a deep crimson to wash his face. The short, shaped brown silk was an exclamation point of accusation, staring him in the face. His quirky mind likened it to a g-string tossed aside in careless abandon. Cursing under his breath, he grabbed the piece of fabric and hastily stuffed it into his pocket.

Just an hour before…no, scratch that, just *yesterday*…he had been a man ruled primarily by his intellect, a man of honor and dignity. And now, a mere twenty-four hours later, he was a…what? Pervert? Sex maniac? Lothario? Lesley held two university degrees, and he couldn't, at this moment, fill in the blank.

It was a good thing, he mused as he opened the screen door, that they were withdrawing to neutral ground. Charlie had said that she lived with her three brothers. The last thing he needed was some big bruiser coming home, finding the two of them there with the scent of sex ripe in the air.

He could hold his own with anyone, but that wouldn't help things right now.

The soft sound of light footsteps snagged his attention. Charlie stood at the base of the stairs, looking as confused and uncomfortable as he felt. Somehow, knowing he wasn't alone in this predicament made the situation marginally better.

They stood for a long moment simply looking at each other. Lesley watched Charlie's eyes approach the weight-lifting bench, then skitter away again. He hadn't needed her verbal protest earlier to know that she wasn't a woman who usually threw herself at men she didn't know. That was a given. He didn't think he had to explain that his behavior over the last hour was out of character, either. He sensed she already knew that much about him.

"Ah...there's a coffee shop over on Forsyth," he said quietly. "They're usually not too busy this time of day. Do you want to ride with me, or take your truck and follow?"

He wasn't surprised when Charlie didn't take the easy way out. She looked him square in the eye when she gave him her answer.

"I'll ride with you. Thanks."

Chapter 4

It was a lot more awkward than he had thought it would be.

Though they had chosen it as neutral ground, the coffee shop itself was familiar to Lesley. There was nothing formulaic about Maxi's. Situated between a residential neighborhood and the industrial district, Maxi's was open seven days a week, six a.m. till ten p.m.

The tables were sturdy, and the chairs were not attached to them. For this alone, Lesley was grateful. At his height, he suffered every time he tried to stuff himself into those one-piece contraptions the chain stores and mall food-courts favored. He and Charlie were of the same mind as, after receiving their cups of coffee, they both walked to the back of the shop. Once seated, he kept his attention on his coffee, feeling awkward and unsure of what came next.

"This is fun," Charlie said at last.

Lesley exhaled deeply. He was being an ass, and he knew it. "Yeah, it is. So I'll go first. I'm not going to apologize for having sex with you."

"I don't expect you to. I don't want you to. And neither will I."

"Good. Moving on, I don't know how to explain what just happened between us. Or, perhaps the better way of saying it is, I can't explain *why*. There's just something about you, Charlie, that gets me…wound up."

"We were standing in your bedroom this morning, and I was thinking, 'This man is *so* not my type, but all I want to do is bounce in his lap.' So I guess we're on the same page, so far. The thing is, Lesley, I don't do one-night stands. I've never done one-night stands."

There were only a couple of other customers in the coffee shop. Even sitting in the back and away from everyone else, they were careful to keep their voices down.

"I don't, either. I know that some men have no difficulty with the concept, or the practice, but that's never been my style. And I generally get to know a woman and make sure there's affection and respect between us before having sex with her." He lifted her hand to his lips and kissed it lightly. "We were both swept up in that storm, Charlie. It was a mutual tempest."

He needed to let her know that what they had done together hadn't diminished his respect for her. It sounded so sexist, even in this new millennium, but old stereotypes held. A man who met a woman and screwed her soon after was virile; a woman who screwed a man under the same circumstances was, at best, 'loose.' Lesley had never agreed with this sort of double standard.

"Lesley, am I the type of woman you generally go for?"

"To be honest with you, no."

"So we're *really* on the same page."

"We are. Let's see how far we can go in this book we seem to be writing together."

"What do you have in mind?"

"Well, it's a little ass-backwards, but why don't we go out on a couple of dates? There has to be something here, between us, something that our subconscious recognizes but hasn't bothered to tell our conscious minds about. Something more than really fantastic sex."

"Really fantastic, huh?"

"Yeah."

Lesley watched as Charlie's face turned crimson and she ducked her head, looking away. He wasn't surprised when, just moments later, she inhaled deeply and made herself look him in the eye. She was, he thought, one gutsy lady.

"Yeah, 'really fantastic' covers it pretty well. I think going out on a couple of dates is a good idea. And since we're on the same page, how about if you choose one, and I choose the other. Then we can decide…well, we can decide if we have a relationship, or not."

"That sounds like a plan."

"There is just one thing, though."

"No more sex."

Charlie's laugh sounded nervous. "At least, not during these first dates. Because…"

"Because if we hit the sheets it would cloud our minds, prevent us from really getting to know each other. We already know we match well sexually."

"You have a talent for understatement."

That's not all Lesley had. As he sat across from Charlie in the coffee shop, he willed his perky penis to lie down and *stay down*. And he wondered how he was going to manage the 'no sex' rule on these dates. If he was this ready to fire after the way he'd just spent the last hour, how the hell was he going to handle being with her and not having her after even a day of abstinence?

* * * *

She forgot to ask him how she should dress.

Charlie was secretly relieved that the stress of choosing entertainment for their first evening out wasn't on her shoulders. She did have to come up with something to do the Saturday after next, though. That was the other thing they had agreed upon: two dates, two Saturdays, a week apart. That way, they'd reasoned, if they decided they were in a relationship, and wound up on the exercise equipment again, they would have known each other for close to three weeks, which was a little more circumspect than, say, three hours.

She could have asked Leslie during the week about their upcoming date, since she was working on his roof. But of course,

May had turned beastly hot. At the end of the day she was too hot, grimy and tired to want him to see her like that, so she hadn't been able to ask him what she should wear for Saturday evening.

In the end, she settled on a short black skirt and a peach colored blouse. On her arm she carried a black jacket with silver pinstripes. If wherever they ended up was a little dressy, she hoped the jacket would add just enough posh to pass muster. With a last check of her hair and make-up in her bedroom mirror, she left the room and walked as silently as she could down the stairs. Discretion had her outside, waiting on the front porch for Lesley. Thanks to their unusual second encounter, she wasn't quite ready to have him meet her brothers, or vice versa.

* * * *

It had worried him at first, and even caused him a bit of sleeplessness. He wasn't used to planning an evening's entertainment for a woman about whom he, basically, knew nothing more than what she did for a living. He wanted to choose something for their first date that Charlie would really like, take her someplace where she would feel at ease, where she could enjoy herself. He had been totally at sea until the 'local events' blurb on the radio gave him an idea. It was the perfect solution, and it was right there on campus!

The evening would be ideal for Charlie, he was certain of it. The venue he had chosen would appeal to anyone who had such a well-equipped home gym in her basement, and might even serve as a reminder of the incredibly hot sex they had shared. As he slid behind the wheel and started his car at ten minutes of seven, he was anticipating a successful evening. Well, he grimaced, successful in that Charlie would have a good time, and they would be one step closer to admitting that they were indeed in a relationship.

He wanted to have sex with her again very, very badly.

Lesley frowned as he negotiated the few miles between his house and hers. He wasn't a sex maniac. 'Scoring' had never been high on his priority list. Yes, he had always looked forward to having sex, enjoyed it immensely. What man didn't? But that had never been the *sole* purpose behind going out on a date before.

He wasn't comfortable thinking that this time, it was. Charlie was a fever in his blood, an itch under his skin begging to be scratched. He wanted to scratch over and over again, and he didn't give a good damn if either of them got raw in the process.

Lesley cursed. Just thinking about getting naked with Charlie had him hard. He quickly turned the radio to full blast, and began singing at the top of his lungs. There was no way he was walking up to Charlie's house, knocking on the door, and facing *any* of her brothers with a hard-on.

He was relieved, but not at all surprised to see Charlie waiting outside, on time, ready to go. No female guile in her, obviously. Her behavior just reinforced his belief that he had chosen the evening's program well. In all probability, candle light and soft music, flowers and flambé would just leave her cold.

* * * *

The evening started out awkward and went straight down hill from there.

"Um…hi," she offered as soon as she got into his car. She took a moment to buckle her seat belt even as she scanned his attire. He was in crisp khaki pants and a beige collared shirt. *No need for the jacket,* she thought as she laid it on her lap. At least they were dressed somewhat the same, which eased one concern.

"Hi. You're…prompt."

At Lesley's compliment, she realized that being ready on the porch could be interpreted as eagerness to get laid. She felt her face heat. All right, so maybe she was really hoping that things would work out between them. As far as she could see, just two evenings out separated her from the fulfillment of her desires.

But at this point she certainly did not want him to know that.

"Um...well, I didn't want to make you wait. And...to be honest, I didn't want you to have to go through whatever gauntlet my brothers might devise."

"You want to keep this just between us, for now?"

"If you don't mind."

"No, I don't mind," he half chuckled his response. "Truth to tell, in light of how we behaved on Monday, I don't mind putting off that meeting for a bit. I have the feeling that any of your brothers would take one look at my face and beat the crap out of me, just on principle."

"No, they're not like that."

Silence enveloped them. After a few moments of feeling fidgety, it occurred to Charlie that she had absolutely no idea what a Director of Library Services *did.*

"So...um...how was your week?"

"It was a good one, thanks."

Charlie kept looking at him, waiting for more. After a moment, he flashed her a quick glance, and a sheepish smile, and continued.

"I spent a great deal of time refining the annual budget for next year, approved the acquisitions list for the next two months, hired two new employees, and finished a round of luncheons with...patrons."

Charlie noticed that they seemed to be driving toward the university. She wondered if talking about his work was somehow responsible for the direction they were headed.

"So, where are we going?" she asked brightly, prepared to be consoling if he realized he was going the wrong way.

"We're in luck. It was the very devil getting tickets at the last minute. I'm not ashamed to say that I was able to pull some strings, since the event is taking place on campus. I've been told we'll have the best seats in the house."

Of all the things Charlie might have guessed that he would do for entertainment, being a spectator at a weight-lifting competition wasn't one of them. In fact, until they arrived at the University gymnasium, she never would have guessed that anyone would.

The place was packed with avid fans. There really wasn't much room in the gymnasium's bleachers, and no back rests for the seats.

The list of competitors was very, very long. From her program she learned that the best of each division would move on to join the National Olympic team. Certainly the athletes and coaches were serious, dedicated individuals, and she understood that to them, this was an important event. For some, it would be the realization of a life-long dream; for others, bitter disappointment and the end of a faithfully traveled road.

It was this perspective that she held onto with both hands and her teeth.

"Yeah, Louie my man! Louie! Louie! Louie!"

Charlie pitched forward as the noisy supporter sitting directly behind her bumped into her as he surged to his feet. Pure luck had her moving her soft drink away from her body so that it didn't spill all over her. Lesley caught her deftly, which she considered amazing considering the trance-like state he'd been in.

"Oops. Careful, there."

Careful there? What, was he so enraptured with the action that he hadn't noticed Bubba behind her? Charlie sent a withering look over her shoulder, but Bubba looked as if he was either trying to take the weight for Louie, or on the verge of having an accident in his pants.

"Yeah! Yeah! *That's* what I'm talking about!"

This time Charlie had the presence of mind to move defensively. She watched as Bubba finally noticed her.

"That's Louie, my cousin. He's gonna win a freaking gold medal."

"Congratulations."

Her entire exchange with the loud man went unnoticed by her date. Since Lesley appeared enraptured, she bit back a groan and did her best to simulate interest. She figured that basic interest was the best she could shoot for. Shoot. Damn, if they *had* to attend a sporting event, why couldn't it have been basketball? The Toronto team was hot this season, and she had been fortunate enough to attend a couple of games so far. She looked from the half eaten over-done hot dog in her hand—dinner—to the staging area. There was a sign posted that tracked the progress of the event. It felt like they had been here forever, but she could see that they were only about of a third of the way done.

"Here comes Jim-bo. This is the putz that always steals Louie's wins. Hope he freaking chokes!"

Charlie responded to the unwanted commentary by moving just a bit closer to Lesley.

"Pretty exciting, isn't it?" Lesley seemed to be waiting eagerly for her response.

"I can honestly say I've never experienced an evening quite like this before in my entire life."

"No way! No way! That's a foul! Get him out of there!" Bubba jumped to his feet once more and narrowly missed knocking Charlie in the head with his knees.

Charlie sighed. It was going to be a long night. She began to yearn to escape.

Chapter 5

Quick, man, think of something, anything, and get us out of here!

Lesley had to tell his inner imp to sit down and *shut up*. Thanks to
that built-in creature of random and dangerous thought, he had damn
near blown it. Still, he had hoped, even as the question left his lips,
that Charlie would indicate that she'd had enough of this mind-
numbing event.

He could pat himself on the back for having chosen the perfect
evening for his date and, conversely, kick himself in the ass for
voluntarily setting himself up for this kind of torture.

It was the most boring evening of his entire life. Blessing his
ability to withdraw into his thoughts, he had spent the last half hour
planning the reorganization of the periodicals section of the library.
Only the realization that he hadn't spoken to Charlie for nearly half an
hour had snapped him out of his daze. When distracted, Lesley had
been accused of appearing to be mesmerized.

There was an aroma that permeated the auditorium, an earthy
scent that Lesley figured was the natural result of having so many
people in a confined space, with bright lights and exertion and
rampant ennui. Could boredom have an odor? He saw that Charlie
was so involved in the event that she had only eaten half of her hot
dog. The other half looked as if it would grow mold within her grasp
at any moment now.

Actually, the hot dogs hadn't been that fresh, and the sodas had
been more than a little watered-down. The menu wasn't his idea of
gourmet fare, but time had been short, and the refreshments sold on-

site. He supposed, though, that he owed it to his date to remind her of the food in her hand, or relieve her of it.

"Are you finished with that?"

He gave her an encouraging smile when she finally focused on him, and his question. Then she looked down to where he was pointing.

"Ah, yeah, I am. Actually, I'm not feeling that well."

Lesley had taken the leftover dinner from her. Now he flashed her a look of concern.

"You should have said something sooner. If you're not well, you really should be at home. In…ah, that is, resting."

"Oh…yes, all right…"

She seemed so hesitant that Lesley guessed she was really beginning to feel out of it.

"Here, let me help you up." He made his movements slow and gentle as he helped her to her feet. Slipping his arm around her, he led her out into the night, pausing to allow her the chance to inhale the fresh air.

"Can you make it to the car, Charlie?"

"Of course. I'm all right, really."

"Not the type to want to be fussed over, huh? I can understand that. But just lean on me, okay? We're almost there."

Lesley was quite aware of the tiny tendrils of guilt that were beginning to swim through his veins. He had wanted the *event* to be over, not the time he was spending with Charlie. It was irrational, but he couldn't help but wonder if her illness was all his fault.

"Here we are," he said as he opened the door of his car and helped her inside, buckling her seat belt. "I'll have you home safe and sound soon. I'm sorry you're not feeling well, Charlie."

* * * *

Charlie felt guilty as hell. She wasn't ill in the least, but if she had to sit through much more of that competition, she was very much afraid that she would be, and violently, too.

It was very sweet, Charlie thought, the way Lesley was being so solicitous of her. He put an arm around her, guiding her out into the night as if she was the most fragile, delicate flower. Tucking her into his car, even doing up her seat belt. It even felt as if he turned the key in the ignition more gently than normal.

"Let me know if you need me to pull over."

"I think I'll be all right."

"You need to get yourself straight to bed. I should come in and make sure there's someone there who can take care of you."

"No, that's not necessary. Really. Chad is home tonight." Charlie *was* beginning to feel ill – sick that she was putting him through such worry, just because she had been a little bored.

"Well, that's good then. You can't be too careful with these sudden attacks of illness. The same thing happened to my Aunt Edith. Two days later, she was gone."

"Your Aunt Edith was in her nineties, wasn't she?"

"Well, yeah. But still. Maybe I should take you to the hospital. It's not that far out of the way."

Charlie felt lower than the lowest slug that slithered and oozed under the rocks in her garden. Here was this sweet, caring man, who also happened to be a terrific lover, fretting over her when there had been nothing at all wrong with her.

"No, really. I'll be fine once I get home. Honest. I'm already feeling a bit better."

"I'll call you when *I* get home, then, just to be certain that you're really all right. Promise me, though, that you'll call the doctor if you aren't completely better by tomorrow."

"I promise."

They had already arrived at Charlie's house. She could see that Chad was indeed home, and likely in the family room at the back of the house watching a movie. The front porch light was off, as she had left it. It was only around ten, really too early to end the evening as far as she was concerned, but she had painted herself into a corner with her own lie. Charlie didn't want to tell him that the venue he had chosen sucked. She would make up for her poor behavior tonight, she promised herself, by being extra-amenable next Saturday.

"I really want to kiss you," Lesley said as he put his arm around her and walked her to the door.

His words spiked her libido, and she looked up to encounter his regretful, wistful expression.

Charlie didn't think, she just reacted. Grabbing his shirtfront with both hands she yanked him to her. She sank into his mouth, forgetting that she wasn't supposed to be feeling well. His tongue did the salsa with hers as his hands went from her shoulders to her back, finally fastening on her ass and pulling her against his erection. She wound her arms around his neck, swallowing his groan when she tried to climb him.

Rational thought ended, and all she could do was feel. When he lifted her off the ground, she wrapped her arms and legs around him and rubbed her pussy against his groin. His groan of delight tasted so good.

Charlie felt the movement of his hand against her crotch, and from the sound of the tear of plastic and the frantic motion of his hands, knew what was coming next. She was deliciously wet by the time she felt the heat of his flesh. Then the stiff rod of his latex-covered penis was nudging aside her panties and he was sliding into her. She broke their kiss just long enough to suck in air and groan. He was so very deep inside her, hot and hard and *wonderful*. She whimpered, a female kind of sound she'd never made before, then grunted in satisfaction when he leaned against the sturdy porch rail.

Not waiting another moment she began to ride up and down on him, reveling in the sensation of his cock sliding in and out of her pussy. At this angle, and driven by her own weight, every downward stroke nudged the tip of him against her cervix.

"Yes!" she cried softly as she felt the gathering explosion, as she felt her vagina contract around him, as her own juices mingled with his semen.

For a long moment, there was only the sound of their heavy breathing. Charlie had rested her head on his shoulder, and she thought it felt so good there. Then he lowered her slowly to her feet, and she looked up at him.

Charlie blinked, coming out of her sexual haze. For a long moment she simply stared at Lesley, wondering why they had stopped, why he hadn't pulled her to the ground and done it all over again. Reality took a few precious seconds to kick in. *Oh yeah,* she thought at last, *the man just brought you home because you ended the date early with a lie about being sick.* It took a few more precious moments for the rest of it to gel in her brain. *Ah, fuck, we weren't going to do that.*

"I don't know what just got into me."

"I did." Then Lesley rested his forehead against hers. "Honest, Charlie, I didn't plan to do that. Hit me, will you? I'm a real asshole for fucking you when you don't feel well."

"You're not an asshole. I have a mouth, I could have said no. But I didn't want to say no. I wanted you."

"Good night, Charlie. I'll call you tomorrow, if that's all right. See how you're feeling?"

Charlie felt guilty that Lesley was feeling guilty, but she didn't know how to make it better. *Shit, what a mess.* Maybe an end to the evening would be the best option. Strategic withdrawal—no pun intended—by all parties.

"Yes...all right. That would be nice. Good night, Lesley."

* * * *

He had to be some kind of lower-than-a-snake's-belly life form to have just rutted with a woman who was ill. Guilt was gnawing big, gaping holes in Lesley Farmer. He thought he could almost qualify for the Olympics himself, judging by the speed with which he'd seized the first opportunity to end the evening. And *then* he had the nerve to fuck her on her front porch. If it weren't for the fact that he was very strongly attracted to the woman, not to mention the near meltdown of the sex, he'd beg off next Saturday's date. His guilt kicked him harder. He couldn't beg off next Saturday, not after the way he had just nailed her and then bailed on her. The date portion of the evening had been a disaster, but to be perfectly honest, *he* had been the one to choose the evening's entertainment in the first place. Considering the intimacy they'd just shared, he owed her, at the very least, another evening out.

He wasn't very proud of the way he'd been behaving this past week. He couldn't even explain his actions to himself. Charlie had aroused him and pissed him off at their first meeting. Thoughts of her had clouded his mind when he was supposed to have been working. They had spilled over into his luncheon with a patron and *that* had almost been a disaster. He decided that the best thing he could do would be to collect the quote, approve the work, and put the vixen out of his mind. But what did he do instead? He behaved like a Lothario, fucking her on the very same day they met, right there on a weightlifting bench, without even looking for a bed. Afterwards, he had faced up to his actions in a civilized manner. He almost gave himself points for that. They went to neutral ground, discussed things rationally, and had agreed that they should get to know each other without the sex.

That plan hadn't fared any better than the first one.

It was time, Lesley decided, to get advice. There had been a few times in his life when the wise words of another—someone removed from the situation—had helped him see what was going on clearly.

Tomorrow, Sunday, he'd run some of this past his best friend…in broad, general terms, of course.

Having outlined the next step to take made him feel marginally better. As he reviewed the evening one more time he couldn't help releasing a frustrated sigh. It was just too bad, he thought as he pulled the car into his own drive, that the woman didn't like basketball. The Raptors had played tonight, and Toronto wasn't so far away as to rule out going to a game.

* * * *

Charlie and her best friend, Megan Elizabeth, had a standing Sunday morning squash date. Neither could hide much from the other. By the end of the second game, Megan knew something was up with her best friend.

"I'm creaming you, and although that is a heady accomplishment not to be underrated, these victories are way too easy for me to wallow in. You're distracted. What's up, girlfriend?"

"I've done something really…hell, I don't even know what to call it! Stupid? Impetuous? Reckless? All of the above? M.E., I've never been so confused in my entire life."

"Let's change and go somewhere else. The UnClub is a great place to play, but a poor place to dish. No chocolate."

It took only twenty minutes for them to shower, change, and drive to a near-by restaurant.

"You have to stop beating yourself up over this, Charlie. There is nothing wrong with two healthy, unattached adults doing the mattress rumba. In fact, I do believe that in this day and age, the activity is even considered *normal*."

Charlie pushed aside the extra large helping of triple chocolate cake she'd ordered.

"This is me, remember? The oldest living virgin in town, or at least I was until Todd Carmichael swept me off my feet five years ago. Six hours, Megan! I'd only known the guy for six hours!"

"It's not the length of time of the association, Charlie, but the quality of the encounter that counts."

Charlie gave her friend a pointed stare. She could see in Megan's eyes that the other woman was reviewing all the information so recently imparted over chocolate. She knew the exact moment Megan came to realize that if one counted the actual time spent in each other's company, that six hours was reduced to less than one.

"Okay, so that isn't a hard and fast rule."

"Balling him Monday was bad enough. But then last night, after the lousy date, after lying about not feeling well, what do I do? I grab him and climb his flagpole. Literally. And yet, he is *so* not my type. I just don't know what to do, M.E." Charlie put her head in her hands, not knowing whether she wanted to scream or cry.

"The sex last night was normal," Megan spoke around her cake. "The real problem is the rotten evening before hand. *That* probably happened because both of you were a little freaked out, you know, doing everything backwards. He never asked you what you'd like to do, because the two of you skipped over the 'getting to know you' part of the relationship-building program."

"Skipped over it?" Charlie flopped back against the seatback and exhaled heavily. "I think we rode a rocket launcher beyond it and into the next county. Or at least I did. This entire thing is not like me at all. Usually I talk with a guy more than a few times, get a pretty good idea of what he's like, what his tastes are, before agreeing to even go out with him. And sex? Well, you know how rarely I've done that." She leaned forward and buried her face in her hands again, as if temporarily hiding would make the madness go away.

"So there's your solution."

Charlie looked up when Megan squeezed her hand. "You arrange to have coffee with this man, and do that kind of chatting now."

"And tell him that I had an absolutely dreadful time last night, so dreadful that I lied to him about being ill? And then I jumped him just for the sex? Are you *crazy*?" Charlie shook her head because this was one of the few times in all the years she'd known her that her best friend just wasn't getting it.

"Well, what's wrong with that?"

"What's wrong with that is the fact that I *haven't* called off next weekend's date despite last night's disaster pretty clearly spells out that I want to have sex with him *again*."

"And that's a problem because…"

"Because…because…it just is, okay? Besides, I've already figured out the perfect date for next Saturday night, since it's my turn to choose." Thinking of those plans now calmed her enough that she took back the cake she'd pushed away.

"Oh boy."

She wasn't going to let Megan Elizabeth's tone dissuade her. "Trust me. I know exactly what I'm doing."

Chapter 6

"My game!" Percy crowed.

"Shit." Lesley spat.

"Now, is that any way for a university executive to talk?"

"Today I'm a university executive. Last week I was just a librarian."

"Yeah, well, last week you beat me."

Lesley couldn't help but laugh. Winded, dripping sweat, he was grateful for the humor. That was one thing he could count on his best friend Percy to provide: a good laugh.

One of the real plusses of relocating and living in the house his aunt had bequeathed to him had been discovering that Percy had come back home to live as well. The two men had hooked up during Lesley's first weekend in town, and had met for squash every Sunday afternoon since.

"There's this black cloud I can see hovering over your head. Let's grab a couple of cold ones in the sports bar and you can tell me all about the life of the lonely librarian."

"Not so lonely this past week," Lesley mumbled.

As they changed and headed to lunch, Percy listened without interruption while Lesley recounted the pertinent events of the last week, beginning with the break and enter tree and ending with the disaster of the night before.

"What kind of a man does that make me? I can hardly wait to have sex with her again but I couldn't be rid of her fast enough before that."

"I'd say that makes you a man, period. We're simple creatures, Lesley, at the heart of it: Feed us, fuck us, and leave us alone."

"That's…sick," Lesley sputtered through his laughter.

"No, that's just what we're all capable of from time to time. What I'm trying to tell you is, don't beat yourself up over this."

"Can't help it," Lesley said as he took a long draught from his beer. "After the way I acted last night, I half expect to find a message on my answering machine when I get home today, telling me to kiss off."

"What you need to do is give the lady a call, arrange to meet her. Go out for coffee, or something, and hash this all out. Be honest with her. Though, in all fairness, that venue last night was *your* choice."

As Lesley watched, a passing blonde snagged Percy's interest. He waited until he had his friend's attention again before continuing. "Which obviously suited her just fine. I have no idea what she's planned for next Saturday, if there is a next Saturday. But I've already made up my mind to be the most attentive, appreciative, appealing date in the history of humankind. And, I'm going to keep my hands, and other body parts, to myself."

Percy shook his head slowly. "Lesley, a man doesn't change his basic nature, no matter how enticing the pheromones. If there's something about this woman that does it for you, there's likely more to the attraction than just the sexual. The problem is, you've skipped all the steps in the getting-to-know-you waltz. What, exactly, did you base your choice on for last night's entertainment?"

Lesley opened his mouth and then snapped it shut again. He'd told Percy the gist of things, but not the details. He'd told him that he'd become intimate with Charlie the same day they met. He hadn't said, *I nailed her right there in her in-home gym, on the weight-lifting bench.*

"There's exercise equipment in her basement."

He tilted his head in response to Percy's pointed stare.

"In the house she shares with her three adult brothers. Gee, imagine that."

That comment gave Lesley pause, but then he shook his head. "I was there last night. You weren't. She was one hundred per cent into that competition. I almost felt de trop, if you know what I mean."

Percy wasn't convinced. "Maybe you're right. But my best advice is still sit down and talk to the woman. Get to know her. We're all of us greater than the sum of our parts."

"You're right." Lesley finished his beer then raised his hand, signaling the waiter. The men always had two beers on Sunday afternoon, the second with lunch.

"There has to be something real and worthwhile between Charlie and me. I just need to be patient, *not* let nature take its course for the next week, and see if we can't discover just what that is."

"My money's on you, pal, 'cause I just don't think you have a future as a Lothario."

"If the way my conscience has been stoning me these last few days is any indication, neither do I."

* * * *

They had dinner at an upscale bistro called the *Wild Carrot*. Situated in one of the renovated town houses at the edge of the park not far from the university, the establishment boasted nouvelle cuisine as well as extensive vegetarian fare and had, Charlie informed Lesley as he parked his car on the quiet street, been written up last week in the local paper.

Lesley was a meat and potatoes man himself. Give him a hunk of beef or a nice piece of chicken or pork, and he was a happy man. But he was not above a little adventure when it came to his palate.

He ordered the medallions of veal, and could do nothing but stare when his meal was served to him. The anticipation he felt when he'd seen the waiter set down the tray with the enormous white plates fled when the silver domed lid was lifted.

The chef thought medallions were the size of quarters, obviously, and had artistically arranged a dollar's worth on the plate. Directly across from the meat were three anemic looking spears of asparagus. Two tiny roasted red potatoes completed the presentation, which had been thoughtfully garnished with one sprig of dill, resembling an inside-out umbrella shading the bare portion of the china.

He'd heard of minimalist art and music. Minimalist cuisine was a new one on him.

Lesley was reasonably certain that Charlie had ordered chicken. But looking at her plate, he honestly couldn't say what it was. He returned her smile when she looked up at him. She seemed more than comfortable in this venue, and he was damned if he'd let his own discomfort show.

There was almost an hour between the end of dinner and the beginning of the event at the museum.

"Want to take a drive through the park?" Lesley asked as he saw her seated in his car.

"That would be nice."

He maneuvered the vehicle into the tree-filled public park. Late afternoon sunlight kissed the sky and the song of birds filled the air. There were only a few people enjoying the evening out of doors, but there were no other cars on the one-way driving track. Here and there as the track wound through the greenery, there were parking areas, usually near picnic tables. The light musky scent of Charlie's perfume teased Lesley's senses as he drove, its allure beating out the scent of flowers wafting into the car window.

He wanted to taste her, just a little. Feeling reasonably confident that a kiss wouldn't get out of hand in the front seat of his car in nearly broad daylight, Lesley pulled the car into a parking spot, killed the engine, and turned to her.

"I want to kiss you."

"I want to kiss you, too."

Their lips met and passion exploded. *This taste of her*, Lesley thought, *was true nourishment*. Groans and pants and tiny curses filled the car. Lesley scooped Charlie up, moved over then settled her so she was straddling his lap. He had her elegant dress around her waist in no time, and his hands were stroking the heated flesh between her thighs.

No panties barred his way. She wore garter and stockings under her skirt, and Lesley knew in that moment he wouldn't be able to stop. It took but a moment to unzip his pants and don protection. His cock slid inside her and they both sighed.

"I wasn't going to do this but I need…"

"Me too, both counts. Damn, Charlie, your pussy feels so good. Squeeze me, baby."

"Like this?" Charlie flexed her inner muscles, and Lesley groaned in ecstasy.

"Just exactly like that."

It didn't take long. Lesley clamped his hands on her hips, helping her to ride his thrusting cock. Fast and hard he moved them both, feeding a hunger that refused to be sated. The rippling of her pussy along his length had him coming hard and long.

The sound of heavy breathing filled the car. Charlie's head was on Lesley's shoulder, and his was back against the top of the seat.

"I swear to you I am *not* a sex maniac."

"Well, for a couple of people who aren't we're giving damn good imitations."

"No kidding. There's just something about us, Charlie. We can't seem to be together alone without…"

"I've noticed that."

"Have you?"

"Rather hard to miss since I keep ending up bouncing on BoBo."

His chuckle jiggled them both. He reached around her, scooping a packet of tissues from the glove box. It took them a few moments to tidy up and put themselves back together. Just before he started the car again, he gave Charlie a fierce hug.

"I'll try to behave myself for the rest of the night."

"Me too. If we succeed, it will be a record."

* * * *

The building was certainly impressive. Concrete and chrome, granite and glass, it gleamed in the setting sun like a golden statue set amongst its plain-Jane brick and mortar neighbors. One of the latest of the urban renewal projects the mavens of society were always boasting on, Lesley had to admit that the structure was pleasing to the eye.

He had never toured the facility. The name, New Age Gallery, in his opinion, said it all. Lesley's tastes in art ran to the more traditional. Give him a Monet or a Turner any day. Pieces of a pick-up truck torn asunder and welded to a steel slab and called art? No thanks. A board with dead bugs pasted in the shape of a butterfly? Not even close. He had promised himself that he would be the perfect date tonight, no matter what. It seemed God had heard him and was likely chuckling now, rubbing His hands together in glee. It wasn't as bad, Lesley conceded, as the weight lifting competition. Sure, he was in a soulless gallery viewing garage sale rejects, drinking cheap wine and having his brain cells murdered by elevator music. But at least his date looked spectacular.

As for that interlude in the car…it had been fantastic, but he wasn't going to think about that.

Lesley turned his attention back to Charlie. Who would have guessed that a woman who appeared so comfortable in coveralls could turn herself out so well? His better Angel gave him a good, swift kick. All right, that was unfair. Charlie couldn't very well go climbing roofs and building houses dressed in a sexy cocktail dress. When his conscience continued to wait impatiently, foot tapping, he acknowledged that where this woman was concerned, he was very guilty of stereotyping. Just one more brick, he mused, to add to the nice little wall of guilt he was building for himself. From start to finish, his behavior with Charlie McKinley had been so completely *not* like the man he truly believed himself to be.

The lights flickered, and he placed a hand on Charlie's back.

"It's time to take our seats."

She blinked a couple of times, before giving him a dazzling smile. "Great! This is really amazing, isn't it?"

"Yes," he agreed honestly. "It's really quite something."

* * * *

If being considered cultured meant you were expected to understand and appreciate exhibits like this, Charlie figured she was doomed to be uncouth for the rest of her life. When she thought of art, she thought of paintings. Not just the renderings of the masters, like some of the canvases that were known universally, but...bowls of fruit. And of course, landscapes.

When had the careless pelting of colors on a board become considered art? Was she uninformed, ignorant, or just hopelessly pedantic? Her sense of humor kicked in as she envisioned a magazine article, a photo of herself and the man beside her, bearing the caption: Can This Relationship Be Saved? There was a gnawing in her belly as she realized the answer: probably not.

All she had to do was look at the way Lesley seem entranced by the displays, the way he fit in with this crowd, to know that here again was another area where they were destined to differ. Yeah, they had terrific mind-blowing bone-rattling sex going for them, but not much else that she could see.

She liked the sensation of his hand on her back as he escorted her to her seat. Just that touch had her blood humming. What did that say about her? So far, the only thing she seemed to have in common with

Lesley Farmer *was* the truly fantastic sex. But you couldn't build a relationship, let alone a life, on just sex.

A life? When had her subconscious decided to leapfrog all the way from justifying spontaneous sexual workouts to thinking in terms of a *lifetime?* She tried not to fidget in the chair. It was the folding sort of plastic and metal tubing contraption that was built for neither comfort nor durability. Then the lights dimmed, and a balding, bespectacled man wearing a tuxedo introduced the mistress of ceremonies, some woman with a hyphenated last name.

"Thank you Mr. Farley, and welcome, *welcome*, friends and fellow patrons of the arts. You all know me as a woman whose very heart and soul has been dedicated, these past years, to the improvement of culture and art in our community, the enlightening of the public consciousness through programs and events that appeal to all walks of life…"

Charlie's expression of interested attention lasted one minute, exactly. It was obvious that Mrs. Something-dash-something was enormously impressed with herself. Without thinking, and in a tiny voice, Charlie whispered, "toot, toot," then immediately cringed and closed her eyes.

She opened them again when a quivering motion beside her snagged her attention. Eyes flashing to Lesley's face, she could see the effort he was exerting not to laugh out loud, even as his shoulders were shaking.

Lesley cleared his throat. "Have pity," he whispered. "It might be the only time all year anyone says anything nice about her."

Charlie caught the first burst of laughter that bubbled up from her gut and swallowed hard. Her eyes watered, but she said nothing as Lesley handed her a neatly folded white handkerchief.

She'd never been on a date with a man who carried a folded and pressed white hankie.

"Thank you."

"You're welcome."

They smiled at each other, conspirators sharing a secret. Then their attention was snagged by applause, and each focused on the stage as a serious looking young man made his way to the microphone.

Charlie suddenly remembered that she'd promised herself she would be the most amenable and attentive of dates. It shouldn't be that difficult to appear interested and entertained for the rest of the evening.

Over the next hour she felt as if God had taken her sincere intention as a personal challenge and was determined to prove her wrong. Before tonight she would have sworn that she was not a woman prone to make judgments. The uncomfortable truth dawned somewhere between the poem about wet, discarded newspaper and the short story entitled *The Adventures of Hughie,* Hughie being an earthworm. She was, after all, a woman who made judgments. There was nothing of poetic value to be found in one page from the Fashion section of the *New York Times* being crumpled, wet with rain, lying in the gutter of a suburban street. And, anthropomorphizing aside, earthworms were incapable of having adventures. She hoped. What was the matter with these people? How could they all sit so attentive, applauding politely, after listening to such drivel?

It slowly came to her that people in the audience were talking softly, that they were getting to their feet, moving around. She wondered, awfully, if she'd somehow fallen asleep. She reached a hand up, checking for drool, sighing in relief when she found none. And then the meaning of the movement around her, of the raising of the house lights, penetrated her partially numb brain.

Hope blossomed in Charlie's heart. She didn't mean to sound as eager as she did, but at this point fine control was beyond her abilities.

"It's over?"

Chapter 7

Charlie prayed for strength when she realized the truth: not the end of the program, only an intermission.

Lesley had offered to fix her a plate from the provided refreshments, but on close inspection they had, to her at least, resembled failed biology experiments. When he suggested that they step outside for a breather instead, she had jumped on the chance to at least taste freedom.

"I…ah…was noticing in the program that all the readings tonight are from contest winners." Charlie made her tone as interested as possible, while secretly wondering if there had been more than one entry in each category of the alleged contest.

"Yes, I read that too. The Classical Conservatory Society for the Celebration of the Written Word's second annual contest. I found it odd they didn't list the judges. Usually, that's something that is given wide advertisement."

Unless they're all too ashamed to admit their association with such an event, Charlie thought darkly. But what she said was, "I imagine it must be a thrill for the winners. To stand up and read their work."

"I've never been comfortable doing that, speaking in front of large crowds. I manage at our staff meetings, but anything larger than that, no thanks," Lesley said.

"Only ever had to do that once, at high school graduation," Charlie commiserated. "I got through it, but I'm glad that it's not something that comes up too often in my line of work."

"Yeah, when you're a teenager, everything seems...more. So, what was it? The reason you had to speak at your high school graduation? Presenting flowers to the principal?"

"No. I was Valedictorian."

* * * *

It was the last reading of the evening that did it. Everything had been going really well, Charlie thought. This wasn't her idea of a great time, but hey, she could be flexible. How often did the city have an event of this nature going on? Not often. Not often, either, for the oiled-muscle group. She was working her way around to the idea that maybe she and Dr. Hottie could have a meaningful relationship, after all. She had almost, *almost* suppressed her conscience that was insisting she was only looking for a way to make this relationship work in order to have some more lip-smacking, brain-scrambling sex. She'd been that close to succeeding.

And then, the final reading.

A short story about the end of spring, which was, Charlie understood as the story progressed, a euphemism for the beginning of adulthood. The main character of the story was a caterpillar destined to be a moth, not a butterfly. Charlie had been half listening, half sneaking a peek at her watch, when the final words of the story washed over her.

"In the end, I knew that I could only be what I was, who I was. The happiness brought on by illusion could be heady, but was always temporary. And come the dawn, reality could never be denied, for the illusion would be washed away by the reflection of my true self."

Is that what she had been doing these last two weeks? Pretending to be something, someone she wasn't? Charlie rubbed the bridge of her nose and knew it was true. She had been so driven by hormones and base need that she'd been willing to do anything for more.

But the truth was, except for the sex, she'd had a miserable time last Saturday. She also thought that this evening's event, with the possible exception of the last reading, was nothing more than a bunch of hooey.

And so, too, she sadly realized as she got to her feet, was the idea that she could have a solid relationship with a man with whom she had, apparently, nothing in common.

"Well, that was interesting." Lesley's words, as they exited the building, called to Charlie's innate honesty.

"No, it wasn't. In fact, it just emphasized what I've always suspected. The initials PhD really do stand for 'piled higher and deeper.'"

"I beg your pardon?"

"Those artsy-crafty types are so full of it. None of the displays I looked at were what I'd consider 'art.' And those readings? The adventures of an earthworm? Give me a break. It's all just pretentious crap, half the people deluded into thinking they're above everyone else, the other half too afraid to admit they don't get it and are just going along for appearances' sake. There's nothing of the real world there, at all."

"And I suppose your definition of the *real world* only includes things that sweat and chew gum and communicate by grunts? That old saw about brains versus brawn—and you figure that anything created by *thinking* instead of by *doing* is just crap? Maybe it's all just beyond your limited comprehension."

Charlie felt every muscle in her body jolt from the insult. "Did you just call me stupid?"

"Honey, if the tool-belt fits."

"Well, then, I guess I'd rather be stupid than a self-serving, self-aggrandizing bag of bullshit."

From Lesley's reaction to that–his back stiffened, his hands fisted–she bet he just itched to pop her one.

"I think, Ms. McKinley," he announced, his tone frosty, "that this concludes the entertainment portion of our evening. I'll take you home now. I also believe this *experiment* of ours has gone on long enough."

"I agree completely, Dr. Farmer. I think we might as well chalk these past two weeks up to some sort of cosmic hormonal burp. I should have known better than to try convince myself that it didn't matter that you weren't my usual type."

"On that we can agree. Do up your seat belt. I'll have you home in ten minutes."

"Not without risking a speeding ticket, you won't."

"Trust me. It would be worth it."

Well, he certainly couldn't get rid of me fast enough, she thought a few minutes later as she sat on the edge of her bed. Now that this episode of mindlessness was behind her, though, things could return to normal and she could relax. In fact, she should be feeling pretty good right about now, as she always did when she knew she had made the right decision.

There was just one small problem. She didn't feel good at all. As a matter of fact, she mused as she headed for a shower, robe in hand, if she didn't know better she'd say she was about to indulge in a marathon crying jag. Instead of feeling good, she felt as if she'd just let something precious slip through her fingers.

"All we really had going for us was sex," she mumbled as she adjusted the water, dropped her clothes, and stepped into the spray. Charlie didn't like what that fact, and these feelings, said about her.

* * * *

Lesley threw his jacket into the chair and raked impatient hands through his hair. How dare she impugn his character that way? How dare she categorize tonight's events as self-serving, self-aggrandizing bullshit? His hands stilled in his hair and he frowned. Well, actually, now that he thought about it, she was right. Not to take anything away from those who were pursuing art as they defined it, but Charlie's assessment really, truly matched his own.

But damn, he hated that she'd in effect pigeonholed him in with that group, without really getting to know him at all. "Piled higher and deeper, indeed," he mumbled as he scooped up his jacket and hung it in the closet.

Didn't you do the same thing? Didn't you take her to that boring competition last week because you thought it would appeal to a woman engaged in a blue-collar occupation? Lesley plopped down onto his bed. Well, hell. He *hated* it when his conscience kicked in and was right. Where was his inner imp now? Smart-mouth bastard was probably hiding out until the storm passed.

Yes, he had to admit, he had done just that. From the moment he'd laid eyes on Charlie McKinley, he had let a prejudice he'd not known he possessed rule his brain. He'd pegged her as gum-chewing, hammer-swinging, brain-deficient being.

Stupid women were not named Valedictorian of their high school graduating class.

Well, it was too late now, this insight. Percy had been right. He should have called her up, invited her to coffee, and come clean with her. It would have been the honest thing to do, and the honorable one, as well. But he'd been so certain he knew what he was doing, he'd brushed off his friend's very good advice.

Lesley grabbed up his robe and headed for the shower. He had the certain feeling that he had just let something rare and special slip through his fingers.

Which, he mused, made him—two PhDs or no—one stupid son-of-a-bitch.

* * * *

"I should have followed your advice, Percy," Lesley concluded somberly the next day. Taking another sip of his beer, he waited for his friend's 'I told you so.' Instead, Percy was giving him a sympathetic look and shaking his head.

"I'm sorry things didn't work out for you and this woman. I really had my fingers crossed for you."

"I appreciate that. But why would you, when you could see so clearly that I was heading in the wrong direction?"

"Because I had the feeling that Charlie really mattered."

"Yeah."

Lesley pushed aside his half-full bottle. That was the problem. He'd had trouble sleeping last night when that very thought—that Charlie *really mattered*—presented itself front and center in his mind.

"I keep going over everything that happened. I thought she was enthralled the week before at that competition, but she could have been as bored out of her tree as I was, and just too polite to say anything. I really screwed up, and right from the very first moment. I assumed that since she was dressed in work clothes and owned a small construction business that she was unfeminine and intellectually...less. And now I'm beginning to see that both of those assumptions were way off base. I'm not feeling very good about myself right now. Not just because I pre-judged her, but also because, all my previous protestations to the contrary, the fact that I could become intimate with a woman under those circumstances tells me that I *am* the kind of guy who would do meaningless sex. I'm actually pretty disgusted with myself."

"The department store at the mall is having a special on hair shirts. We could get you one."

"You're supposed to be agreeing with me here, not making fun of me."

"You made a mistake. It happens. You're not perfect, just human like the rest of us. And then, as your best friend, I'm going to state the obvious."

Percy stopped speaking while the waitress delivered their plates of lasagna and salad.

"The obvious?" Lesley prompted.

"The woman is still going to be working on your roof, right?"

"Of course. At least, I hope she is." The thought played through his mind for a moment. "No, of course she is. She's a professional and would never let anything personal get in the way of business." He hoped he was right. It would be hell to have to find someone else to finish a job that had already been started. Besides, he wanted Charlie to have his business. All things considered, it seemed like the least he could do for her.

"So she's still going to be around. You don't have to write this relationship off, Les. Give it another shot. Flowers and an apology should do the trick."

"I don't know, Percy." Lesley forked over his food in an absent way. "Something about Charlie tells me she isn't the forgiving sort."

Percy blinked and shot his friend a disbelieving look. Then, shaking his head and trying not to laugh, he replied, "Well, I'm glad you've learned your lesson and are not going to make any more assumptions where the lady is concerned. Good for you, champ. Good for you."

* * * *

"So that is that. Over. Ruined. Kaput."

"Maybe it's not as bad as you think."

She sat up straight and began to count on her fingers. "I judged him based on what he was wearing, for heaven's sake, and on the basis of his career. I jumped all over him as if he was the poster boy for everyone who has ever ragged on me because I chose not to go to university. And, to top it all off, I apparently *am* the kind of woman who will indulge in a cheap, meaningless affair. That's three strikes! I am so absolutely disgusted with myself."

Charlie laid her head on her arms even as her fists lightly pounded the table. "You know what the kicker is? We were having a pretty good time last night when we weren't so...focused on trying to have a good time. And if he was so wrong for me, I should be feeling great that I've blown him off and I'm never going to see him again. But I don't. I don't feel good about any of it."

She groaned as she laid her head back down and began pounding on the table again.

"He really got to you, huh?"

"Yeah. There was just something about him. And stop snickering. I was *not* referring to his penis, as wonderful as that is. I can't even tell you what it is about him that really clicked for me. But last night, when we were sharing that joke, and he smiled at me...I felt it all the way down to my toes. And now...it's just a mess."

"It's just too bad," Megan sighed heavily, "that you'll never see the man, or work on his roof, ever, ever again. What a shame!"

"I'm still going to finish his roof. That has nothing to do with...with this," Charlie said, waving her hand to indicate her present predicament. "I would never let personal considerations prevent me from honoring a business commitment."

"Well, then, what's the problem? You buy him some flowers, tell him what a complete ass you've been, and ask him to forgive you. Then you jump his bones again."

Charlie's face colored. "I'm not altogether certain that he's the forgiving kind of guy. He couldn't get rid of me fast enough last night. He was going way over the speed limit on Main Street. If a cop had seen him, it would have been bye-bye license."

"Just sounds like he was mad. And from what you told me, I don't think you can blame him for that."

"No," Charlie replied, grudging agreement. She swallowed the lump in her throat. Megan was looking at her expecting complete agreement. Charlie knew that she really did owe Lesley an apology. And flowers? She guessed she'd only feel a little idiotic toting posies over to the man. Damn, she *hated* this new millennium. Equal rights were fine in some things, but this making the first move idea she wasn't so certain about. Whatever happened to the fifties? Of course, she hadn't been alive then, but from what she'd heard the gentleman was the one to make all the first moves—and thereby surely be the first apologize.

"I guess it's up to you," Megan said softly. "Just how much does a second chance with Lesley Farmer mean to you?"

Charlie's response was to groan even more deeply as she laid her head down on the table once more.

Chapter 8

"What do you mean you haven't seen her?"

Lesley shot his friend a sharp look. "I wouldn't have expected to see Charlie up there hammering on shingles, not with the rain we've had since Tuesday."

"So does that mean you haven't had a chance to apologize to her?"

Lesley turned from viewing the items that would soon be auctioned to look at Percy.

"I haven't, no. And the longer I wait, to be honest with you, the more impossible the entire situation seems."

"I never would have thought that you were the sort to shrink away from the difficult."

"Well, ouch." They stopped to look at the table full of antique teddy bears that were being offered, collectively, as one item. Lesley couldn't help but smile. "I should bid on these and then wrap them up and send them to my parents for Christmas."

"Now that sounds Freudian."

"It is. A payback for the fact that I was never permitted any 'toy' that did not serve the higher purpose of preparing me for my future as a great scholar."

"Well, despite that handicap, you turned out all right, except for being an extremely anal, conclusion-jumping nerd who won't swallow his pride to win the hand of the woman he loves."

"Love? Love? I never said I was in love with Charlie."

"Not in words, no. But are you going to stand there and tell me that you're not?"

"No. I'm going to go across the hall. They have a Margaret Lynwood Sawyer over there and I want to get a better look at it."

Percy followed him, snagging two glasses of wine from a passing waiter on the way. There wasn't anything listed in the catalogue for this charity auction that interested Percy nearly as much as needling his best friend did.

"Not only cowardice, but denial. This just gets better and better. And what the hell is a Margaret Lynwood Sawyer?"

"Maybe it was just a case of lust after all. I've been thinking about it almost constantly since last Sunday, when we talked. I really hate to believe that I am so shallow, so...well, *cheap* as to have given in to basic urges like a gigolo. But maybe that's just what happened. Maybe the whole point of this entire affair was to teach me that I *could* be just as low and base a creature as the next man. Maybe the best thing I can do is just move on."

"This," he continued, determined to change the subject and indicating the painting before them, "is a Margaret Lynwood Sawyer. And it's magnificent."

"It's a field, and a stream, and some pine forest."

"Percy, Percy, Percy. A painting is so much more than the sum of its parts."

"All right, *Doctor* Farmer, why don't you educate me?"

"When I was ten, during my third summer here with Aunt Edith, she took me to an outdoor flea market. That is where I saw my first Margaret Lynwood Sawyer. My Aunt Edith met her when she was a girl. The lady had a difficult life, her art having been her only joy and freedom. The paintings aren't valuable, per se. I don't know if there are more than a few dozen people who know her story. You're right, as 'art' they aren't very good. But I always liked her landscapes that were all painted from memories of her childhood."

"And as you grew up, she became a symbol of individuality against the pressure your parents exerted on you to follow in their archeological footsteps?"

Lesley blinked at his friend. "Ah, no. I just really like her paintings."

"You, my friend, are not an open book."

"So I have been told. Let's go grab our seats. I want to sit on the far left, so I can see the pieces as they're brought to the stage. The auction will begin in about twenty minutes, and I want to study the program one more time."

* * * *

"All right, I understand perfectly that with the weather this week, you haven't been able to go over to his house during the day and work on his roof. But hey, they have a whole *other* block of time every twenty-four hours called *the evening*. Since you know where he lives, you could have gone over then and apologized."

Charlie looked at Megan Elizabeth for a long moment. "You know, you can be such a smart ass sometimes."

"I know. But be honest, girlfriend, isn't that one of the things you love best about me?"

"It is, when it's directed elsewhere."

"Seriously, Charlie, after last Sunday, I thought you had made up your mind to go and apologize to the Doc for being such a jerk, and try to start over. So, what happened between then and now?"

"Nothing. I've just had time to think, is all."

"Charlie, thinking is never good for you. Because you don't just think, you *over* think."

"Maybe, in the past, I've been guilty of that from time to time. But not this time."

They stopped at a table full of curios and Charlie found herself frowning. "You know, if you fill your house with these things, you become a slave to the dust rag."

"But they're pretty."

"Pretty useless."

"Well, I'm going to bid on them. I'd like to bid on the teddy bears, but I have a feeling some collector is going to scoop them up."

"I'm saving all my 'bidding power' for that landscape."

"That old thing? It should go cheap. It's junk."

"Megan Elizabeth, just because it doesn't have a famous name on the bottom of it doesn't mean it's junk. Besides, I already have two Margaret Lynwood Sawyers in my collection."

"Your collection?"

"Okay, that sounded officious. I have two of her landscapes, they're in the attic at home, carefully stored against the day I finally move into my own house."

"How come this is the first I'm hearing about this? I thought we were friends."

"We are. I didn't realize that you didn't know I liked this particular artist. Honestly, you don't often see her work up for sale. Someone must have had a screw loose giving it up for charity. But hey, their loss is my gain."

"What's so special about her, anyway?"

"She was a rebel back in the days when women couldn't openly rebel against their parents or husbands. She went through the paces of conformity but found her real 'life' in her art. They're all landscapes, and all painted from her memories from when she was a child. And…I just like them."

"Well, I guess if you're going to spend the rest of your life as a lonely, dried up old spinster because you can't even bring yourself to apologize to the hunk of your dreams when you screw up, you might as well surround yourself with the material things you like."

"Wow. That was good, even for you, M.E. Let's go grab our seats. I want to sit on the far right so I can head straight for the accounts table as soon as I buy that painting."

* * * *

"Item seventeen is an untitled landscape by a minor Ontario artist, M.L. Sawyer. Donated by Mrs. Evelyn Smith. This is one of only twenty landscapes by this artist known to exist. Opening bid is ten dollars. Do I have ten dollars…thank you, number thirty-five…fifteen…number sixty-two…twenty…thank you…twenty-five…twenty-five is bid do I have thirty? Thirty-five do I have forty?"

"One fifty!"

"Charlie, are you nuts? That painting isn't worth…"

"It is to me. Who the hell is bidding against me?"

"Some dark haired hunk with a real scowl on his face."

"Two hundred," the masculine voice retaliated.

"Two-fifty."

"Charlie, you are way too competitive to be here, you know that, don't you? Let the darn thing go before you go over your budget."

"I already *am* over my budget. But I can manage if the bidding doesn't go too much higher."

"I have two fifty from the lady holding number sixty-two. Do I have two sixty?"

"Five hundred!"

"Madame?" The auctioneer was looking for a counter-bid. Charlie turned her shocked eyes away from Lesley and faced the auctioneer. She shook her head 'no' and laid her paddle down.

"Five hundred, once, twice…*Sold*, to the gentleman holding number thirty-five. The Children's Foundation thanks you for your generosity. Now, on to item eighteen…"

* * * *

"You don't look happy about winning," Percy commented as Lesley sank back into his chair.

"That was Charlie. How the hell did she know I wanted that painting, and why would she bid against me?"

Percy shook his head and chuckled. "Here's an idea. Maybe she's thinking the same thing about you right now. Why not go over and find out?"

"Don't think I won't," Lesley bit out as he got to his feet and moved to the aisle. But by the time he made it around the back and up the other side of the audience, Charlie was gone.

* * * *

"Can you believe the nerve of that man? He must have seen me place the first bid and decided to steal my painting just to spite me!"

In nearly forty-eight hours, Charlie still hadn't come down from her mad. She had been so angry that she'd started muttering to her brother Chad in the car as they made their way to Toronto. A couple of questions later, and she told her oldest brother what she had sworn not to tell another soul. If Chad was shocked that she'd had sex with a man she barely knew, he kept it to himself.

"Honey, it could very well be that he wanted the painting on its own merit. That would mean that you have at least two things in common with him."

"Ha ha, very funny. Aren't you even outraged that I...that we..."

"Why the hell should I be? It sounds to me as if the frenzy was mutual. No, you're a big girl, and certainly old enough to do as you choose. And, for the record, I'm with Megan. You need to apologize. Take it from one who knows. Pride can rob you of the chance to be happy."

"Are you still upset over your break-up with Ted?"

"Yeah. Worst mistake of my life. He took a promotion last month and moved to California. I've heard he's already met someone."

"I'm so sorry, bro."

"So am I, baby sister. And I'm just worried that you're making the same mistake with your Lesley."

"He's not *my* Lesley."

* * * *

The action was fast and furious from the get go, and Charlie found herself, as always, completely absorbed in the game. Close to the end of the first half, the home team was up by two points when Kiefer, the all-star forward, pivoted sharply and was about to spring up for a three point attempt when one of the opposing guards got a bit too close, and the ref didn't call it.

"What, are you blind? That was a foul, you idiot! Call it!"

Charlie was by no means the only fan on her feet screaming for the head of the referee. But for whatever reason, she was the *one* fan the cameras found and flashed on the jumbotron. She frowned up at her own image. Scowling, she swung her glance away. She would never know what trick of karma had her eyes skimming the seats on the other side of the court. But they did, and she jolted when they fixed on a seat just down a couple rows and to the left.

"Son of a..."

Chad's arm came around her at the same time her gaze locked with Lesley's. She saw him stiffen, and then turn away.

"What is it, honey?"

Charlie felt her insides melt just a little.

"I think I'm going to have to seriously consider that apology after all," she confessed.

Chapter 9

"Certainly didn't take her any time to jump right back into the game."

"Yes, it was a great game. Our team lives!" Percy's enthusiastic outburst was in stark counterpoint to Lesley's aggravated grumble.

Lesley shot his friend an annoyed look. "Do you mind? I'm suffering here!"

"I do mind if you suffer, but there's nothing I can do about it, is there? Especially when you consistently ignore not only my opinions, but my very excellent advice."

Lesley got into the car, fastened his seat belt, and turned his attention to Percy. "Usually, your advice *is* gold. But in this situation, you've been way off base."

"Says *you*. Because you're so wrapped up in your own fears and insecurities, you can't seem to open your eyes and see what *is*."

"Did you even look at them? Every time our team scored they were hugging or kissing or groping each other."

"Kissing? Groping?"

"Well, they might as well have been. You could tell just by they way they were sitting there that they were awfully *close* to each other. He seemed very protective of her, too."

"The kind of closeness that comes from months, or years, instead of days, wouldn't you say?"

"Now what are you trying to tell me?"

"Maybe they were just friends."

"Yeah, right."

"Hey," Percy shot back, "maybe she looked over at you and me and thought the same things about us."

Lesley blinked at the absurdity of the thought and then burst out laughing.

"In this day and age, the idea isn't that far fetched," Percy defended.

"No, it isn't."

"Lesley, if she's that important to you, I think you ought to follow my original advice. Talk to the woman."

"Yeah. She seems to be that important to me, judging by my reaction to seeing her tonight with another man. So, maybe I will."

But it wasn't for lack of trying on Lesley's part that his plans that week didn't gel. He had meeting on top of meeting over the next four days as funding cuts were announced to the post-secondary education sector, leaving every institution—and therefore every department within every institution—scrambling for the life blood of twenty-first century learning: cash.

As the work on his roof progressed, he began to worry that Charlie would soon be out of his life forever. He would have gone over to her house, but he didn't feel as if a straight out frontal assault would work. At least that's what he told himself, and his prevarication had nothing to do with the fact that Charlie lived with three grown men who were also her brothers, and quite likely to beat the living crap out of him.

On Thursday morning, as he was getting ready to head into work earlier than usual, and struggling with the finicky bathroom plumbing longer than he deemed necessary, he had a brainstorm. He called Mrs. Crosby, and told her what he had in mind. As he got into his car and headed to the university, Lesley had a smile on his face for the first time that week.

* * * *

Charlie frowned as she got out of her truck and her eyes scanned Lesley's driveway. *Damn it!* She had been certain that he didn't leave for work on any given day before seven-thirty. Here she was, seven-fifteen, an hour ahead of her usual time, and the damn man didn't even have the decency to be home! The early bird may get the worm, but Charlie took this occasion to remember that the early worm got eaten.

She didn't think she could, in all good conscience, drag this job out much longer. It was Thursday, and even Tom was beginning to shoot her puzzled looks. She paid him by the hour, and Charlie's extension of the time frame here was eating into her profits, such as they were.

"Yooooo hooooo, Charlieeeee!"

Mrs. Crosby was standing just inside her front door, waving something to get her attention. Charlie waved back and then continued to fasten her tool belt as she headed over to the woman.

"Good morning, Mrs. C."

"Good morning, Charlie. My goodness, you're early today."

"Well, you know what they say. The early bird gets the worm."

"I could never understand that saying. Hate worms, myself. Always have."

Charlie chuckled, even as the elderly woman stood back in silent invitation for her to enter.

"What can I do for you, Mrs. C?"

"Well, I told that nice Dr. Farmer when he called this morning that I would try and deliver his message, but it is my Bridge day, and I wasn't altogether certain that I would be able to know when you arrived, or when you were working, and I certainly did feel badly about the idea of calling you down off that roof. That is such a long way up, isn't it? But then just as I opened my door to look for my morning paper, there you were!"

Charlie had become fluent in *Mrs. C* by now. "Yes, that was good timing. What message do you have for me from Dr. Farmer?"

"Well, come in child. I've just finished brewing my tea, would you like some?"

"No, thank you." Knowing it was useless to protest, Charlie unlaced her work boots, took them off and set them beside the door before following the woman into her kitchen.

"Well, it was just like I was always telling Edith. Edith, I'd say, you need to stay on top of these little jobs, or else they become big jobs and big headaches. That's what my George always said, God rest him. Why, he was always taking himself off to different home shows, going every week to this big building supply store or that one for hours and hours, keeping abreast of all the latest gadgets and do-dads and whatnots that a homeowner needs to be able to keep his home in tip-top condition. Now, I certainly never thought that Edith should do as such, but still, she might have paid a little more attention and hired in folks when things began to go amiss."

Charlie stood and watched as Mrs. Crosby poured herself some tea, added cream and sugar, then took a pastry out of a box and set it on a saucer. She halted in her monologue just long enough to take a bite of her breakfast.

Charlie saw her chance and took it. "What was the message, Mrs. C?"

"The message? Oh, my goodness, the message! Of course, here I am, just going on and on when…I wrote it down…" She quickly sorted through a small stack of papers at the edge of her placemat and just under the wall phone.

"Here it is. Dr. Farmer wants a new upstairs bathroom. Plumbing, fixtures, floor, the works. He wondered if you would have time to give him an estimate, today or tomorrow." She handed the note over to Charlie. "Edith used to complain something awful about her shower being temperamental. I guess Dr. Farmer is more like my George."

Charlie looked at the note and her professional façade nearly cracked. She felt like doing handsprings. Replacing the bathroom would take a good bit of time – depending. She didn't even feel guilty when she realized that the *depending* had more to do with her luck encountering her client face to face than it did anything else.

* * * *

Lesley had been to *The Rumba* a few times since moving into Aunt Edith's house several months before. He and Percy had hit it the first weekend they'd connected again. The music was good, varied, and not too loud. The crowd tended to be late twenties, early thirties, which in turn made for a more congenial evening than, say, frequenting one of the trendier and younger night spots. Fights hardly ever broke out at *The Rumba*. He had been the one to suggest the club tonight as a celebration of Percy's thirty-fifth birthday. Percy had invited two other old friends, Willa and Gordon, to join them.

"Come on, Les, it's easy." Willa was coaxing him to join her on the dance floor. A sexy rhythm was pounding out of the speakers, and she was trying to entice him into holding her closer so she could show him how to move to the beat.

"No way, Will. If I get close to you while you're doing *that* with your hips, your husband is going to kill me."

"True," Gordon laughed. "Lesley is an intelligent man. He can learn everything he needs to know about Latin dancing—or this area's version of it—by watching us." Lesley took the vacated chair and watched the couple move onto the dance floor.

"Reminds me of having sex," Percy said as his eyes scanned the crowd, looking for a likely dance partner. Most often, couples came to *The Rumba*, but there was usually a good mix of singles, too.

"Tell me about it," Lesley hissed, and turned his attention away from the dancers to the drink in his hand.

Watching the gyrating couples reminded him of being with Charlie. Together, they had the same sense of rhythm, like two halves of one whole, fluid and sensual. He took a deep draught of his beer.

At least there was still hope. She'd left a note that she would have an estimate on replacing his bathroom for him on Monday. And on Monday, come hell or high water, he was going to sit down with her and talk. He didn't know what else to do. He couldn't get the damn woman out of his thoughts.

"Lesley."

He looked up to encounter Percy's serious expression. "I know what you can give me for my birthday."

"We agreed no presents this year, for either of us. Remember?"

"I've changed my mind." He nodded toward the other side of the room. Lesley followed his lead, looked, then swore softly.

"If you don't make a move *right now*, I am going to be very disappointed in you. I'll catch a ride home with Will and Gord."

She was with the same guy she'd gone to the game with, and one other man. They all three turned at the same moment, and Lesley realized in a flash of insight that he was a complete idiot. The three looked enough alike to be brothers and sister. One song ended and another began, the beat of this one just as heavy and sensual as the last. Lesley got to his feet slowly and imagined himself a lion stalking his prey. His gaze connected with Charlie's, and he felt his grin turn feral. She froze, not unlike a deer caught in the throes of *fight or flight*.

* * * *

"Hmmm, this is interesting. I'd say the man has decided to take matters into his own hands." Chad couldn't stop the grin. He watched his sister's eyes widen, and noticed the way her breathing had suddenly hitched. He turned his attention to his brother, Carl, laying a hand on his arm to get his attention. He shook his head 'no' slightly as Lesley stopped just inches in front of Charlie.

Charlie felt the rhythm of the music pulsate inside her. She couldn't look away from the chocolate brown eyes that were pinning her in place. Her fingers curled around the hand that caressed then took hold of hers, and her body moved forward in response to the inexorable pull. Standing at the very edge of the dance floor, she placed her hands on his shoulders, and then linked them around his neck. His hands pulled her hips into his. With the music, they began to move as one, as if each sway and dip had been choreographed, each undulation timed and practiced.

One male hand left the safe territory of hip and splayed across a heated, female bottom. One feminine hand began to caress neck and scalp, curling around in unmistakable invitation. Chest to breast and groin to groin, they were as one, wrapped in the sensual haze of the music.

"Can you think of a single reason why you shouldn't come home with me, right now, where we can finish this in my bed?"

Everything inside Charlie had melted, and was heating as if ignited by flame. Parts of her that had felt disjointed and out of sorts were whole again. *This was right.* No matter what logic dictated or social mores proclaimed, this was right. Embolden by the music and the man, Charlie leaned into him, used her tongue to taste his ear lobe and whispered two words.

"Fuck me."

Chapter 10

Each time before, it had been a burning hunger, an overpowering craving to taste that which was considered forbidden, a craving that destroyed all sensibilities in its quest for satiation, a frenzy of uncontrolled feeding. Now, it evolved into an appetite that demanded intricate attention to detail, a need to enhance what was already a keen taste. It demanded to be savored.

The ride in his car seemed endless, enveloped as they were by silent anticipation. Charlie wouldn't have been surprised if he had hauled her over his shoulder, thrown her onto the bed and ravished her as he had before. And she would have ravished him right back, for that was familiar. It was what she had been certain was going to happen, based on the blatant declarations made on the dance floor. Instead, he had held out his hand, led her in and then up. Turning her into his arms he kissed her thoroughly and tenderly. Tongues danced their own version of the Salsa, touching and tasting, sliding and gliding to lap up every nuance of flavor. His hands had trembled as he caressed her back and arms, as if he was afraid to frighten her away or, more, she thought, as if he couldn't quite believe that she was really there, now, with him.

They undressed each other with gentle touches, sweet, savory kisses and reverent caresses. Charlie had been prepared for the inferno, yet the slowly building fire left her shaken. There was nothing to anchor onto here, nothing to grab and make happen. Lesley was so ardent in his lovemaking that she could do nothing but take what he gave her. He had demanded that of her the first time, verbally, and she'd surrendered to him. This time his demand was no less insistent and all the more compelling, for he flooded her with sensation. Her surrender, when it happened, was no less unconditional or complete.

She could never have guessed that a nibble on the tiny area beneath her ear could arouse her so thoroughly, or that her breasts, petted, pinched, then suckled could bring her to orgasm. Having come once, she was saturated again and again until there was nothing left for her to do but lay totally open to him. He could have done anything to her at that point, anything at all, and she wouldn't have been able to stop him. His lovemaking enslaved her completely.

She barely noticed when he paused, just long enough to slip on a condom.

"Take me inside you, Charlie. Let's be one, together."

"*Lesley.* Yes, I want you inside me."

Charlie used the last of her strength to wrap her arms around him as she felt him enter her. The sensation of his cock sliding inside her made her shiver. She enfolded him and squeezed gently, and the arousal bit deep, cried for urgency. But he set the pace, a slow, poignant rhythm. As she spread herself wider for him, tilting her hips in a more complete submission, he did more than touch the edge of her womb; he caressed the edges of her heart. When he placed a hand under her, bringing her closer still, and when his lips found hers and his tongue stroked, enticing her own to join in that same quiet cadence, Charlie felt herself shatter into a million pieces. Her orgasm was rich and deep and so moving that tears leaked, unbidden and unwanted, from her closed eyes.

"It's as if your pussy is drinking from my cock, Charlie, the way your muscles are caressing me."

"Oh God!" His words spiked her orgasm higher, and all she could do was wrap herself around him and let the shattering continue to her very soul.

Later, much later, as she laid awake in the dark, the steady beat of his heart in her ear, she wondered, almost fatally, if she would ever be able to put herself back together again. And if she did, would she ever be whole without him?

* * * *

Waking up alone pissed him off. He didn't need to get out of the bed and search the house to know that Charlie wasn't there. He sensed her absence the way, he imagined, a wolf sensed the absence of its mate. Without opening his eyes, he allowed himself to wallow for a few moments in the wonder of the night before. The sense that came clearer than all the rest was flavor. Lesley couldn't get enough of the taste of her. She was spiced and erotic, aromatic and addictive. He had lapped with his tongue and nibbled with his teeth, and he knew that the flavor of her neck was subtly different from the piquancy of her nipples. Those buds beaded hard in response to his oral stimulation, and as he drew them deep into his mouth, he wondered at the taste of the nectar they would one day release. His arousal had spiked then, the flash of the image in his mind so sharp, so magnetic, that it took every ounce of his will not to take her *right then* and make it so. Had he ever felt driven to plant his seed before now? Not once, even as he admitted deep down inside that a family of his own—a wife and children—was one of his most cherished dreams.

Had he ever felt such softness covering strength in a woman's body before? Had he ever imagined, whimsically, that he could happily spend every moment of every day of the rest of his life immersed in another? Was this, finally, *finally* what love was?

As he flung the blankets back, he let the implications of that thought echo in his mind. He swung his legs off the bed and swore when his feet hit, hard and way too soon, against the floor. It took a moment for the unnatural angle of the bed to identify itself in his brain. Then he recalled, sometime after two in the morning, that he and Charlie had awakened together, turned to each other and…ignited.

A feminine whimper. A masculine chuckle. A package being opened, and more teasing.

"You want more than my fingers in your pussy?"

"Yes. I need your cock."

"Beg."

"Bastard. Fuck that. Fuck *me*." Charlie pushed the hands away that were holding her and mounted him. She laughed aloud at his hiss as she impaled herself. The she rode him hard and fast.

Rearing up, Lesley had deftly flipped their positions, slammed her down onto the bed, splayed her legs wide with his arms, and pounded into her, hard and deep. His cock was impossibly rigid, impossibly hot, and still he fucked her fast and furiously.

It was a war as much as it was sex, where the victors and the vanquished were one.

None of the finesse of earlier in the evening was in evidence as they continued to devour each other. The starving, grasping, pounding romp had left them both sliding almost instantly into the depths of slumber as orgasms faded, sometime immediately after the old four-poster bed had broken. *Is that why she left? Did I hurt her?* Confusion only lasted a moment. No, they had awakened again, just at the edge of dawn. Half asleep, neither used to finding another in their bed, they had touched and petted, sipped and savored. They had come together with tenderness, with a stirring sweetness that Lesley hadn't known he was capable of. He had told her that, in the pre-dawn quiet. He told her that, and much more.

I think I've been waiting a lifetime for you, Charlie.

Well, hell, he thought now as he ran a hand through his already tousled hair. He figured Charlie was a lot of things, but commitment-shy wasn't one of them.

He showered, and the heat of the water caught the scent of her that clung to his skin, as if she were standing under the spray with him. He laughed, a guttural sound, in response to the hard-on he immediately sprouted. He would have enjoyed the opportunity to make her breakfast. Hell, he would have enjoyed the opportunity to have *her* for breakfast.

He had already considered, and discarded, going to her. She had pulled a panicked withdrawal, and he'd allow her that, for now. But he also figured Charlie would be expecting him to show up, or call today or tomorrow.

He was going to do neither. *Damned* if he would be predictable.

She'd promised him an estimate for a new bathroom on Monday. He'd tell her to go ahead with the work, and then, later—probably Tuesday if he could hold out that long—he'd corner her. She could retreat for the moment if she had to, but there was no way in hell he was going to let her run away.

* * * *

Charlie crept into the house. It was just shy of six a.m., and if she was really lucky, everyone was still asleep. She could sneak upstairs, get into her room, and then—hey, who was to say she'd stayed out all night?

It wasn't that she was uncomfortable with the idea of any of her brothers knowing she'd had sex with Lesley. The problem was, appearing so early after spending the night with a man would only raise questions she wasn't certain she was prepared to answer.

Like, why did you sneak out of your lover's bed before he even woke up? Was he brash, cavalier, uncaring?

I think I've been waiting a lifetime for you, Charlie.

Beautiful words. Lovely words. Words many women would thrill to hear. *So what the hell is the matter with me?*

Charlie hadn't spent a lot of time thinking about the future. She had always assumed that she would, of course, eventually find herself in love with someone. When the time was right and when she was ready, she would carefully choose the man with whom she would fall in love and build a life.

It had never occurred to her that she would fall in love without her conscious consent. She wasn't any where *near* ready for that.

She prepared to breathe a sigh of relief as her hand gripped the doorknob to her bedroom and stealthily began to turn it.

"Ahem."

Charlie froze. Peering over her shoulder she scowled at Chad.

"Do I sneak around spying on *you*?"

"No, but then I have the good grace to stay where I am at least until breakfast. So, what happened? Did Marion the librarian boot you out?"

"His name is Lesley, and he certainly did not boot me out."

"Ah, then you must have taken a powder. Crept from his bed before the crack of dawn. Left the poor dear man to wake up, deserted and alone. Do you have any idea how terribly déclassé it is to run off on a lover that way? Not to mention just plain poor manners. What would mother say? Ah, scrap that last thought."

"Whose side are you on, anyway?"

"I am always, dear sister, on your side. Come on down to the kitchen. I'll make you crepes and you can tell me what's bothering you."

"What makes you think something is bothering me?"

"You've been chewing on your bottom lip, honey. It's always a dead giveaway."

* * * *

"So let me get this straight. You think you might be falling in love with the guy, and you're pretty certain he feels the same way about you."

"Right."

"And…"

"What do you mean, 'and'? Isn't that enough?"

"And this is a problem because…."

"It just is, that's all."

"Uh huh."

Rarely had Charlie heard two syllables spoken with such an air of impatient pity. She chanced a peek at her brother's face.

"What?" Was she some brainless moron to deserve such a look from her own brother?

"You can be such a brainless moron sometimes," Chad said as he got up and re-filled their coffee cups.

The scowl she sent him left no room for filial compassion.

"The problem with you, *Charlene*, is that you think you need to be in control of *every damn thing, all the time*. But the thing about love is this: you're never really in control at *any* time. At least not when it comes to who you love and when you fall. No one is."

"But…it's way too soon…"

"To know that you're in love? No such thing as way too soon, baby sister. It's probably way too soon to go to the Bay and register china patterns, but you fall in love in an instant. And Charlie? If you turn your back on this special gift, you'll never forget it, and never stop being sorry—not for the rest of your life."

* * * *

Charlie spent the weekend going from high to low, mood-wise. It was an irritating thing, because she wasn't normally a moody person. By the time Sunday night rolled around she was a nervous wreck from the adrenaline rush that had come with each ring of the telephone. Except for a couple of hours to play squash, she hadn't left the house, so certain was she that if she did, she'd miss Lesley's call. Only, he never called. As she showered and prepared to make it an early night, she didn't think she'd like being in love much if it continued to scramble her brain this way. She felt off balance, out of control, and very, very needy. She needed to hear him, see him, touch him. It was driving her nuts.

So, fine, she couldn't help it if she fell in love with Lesley Farmer. And, since she felt that way about him, it probably *was* a pretty good thing that he seemed to feel the same way about her. She wasn't going to sit around with big sad cow eyes and wait for the phone to ring, at least not after tonight, she quickly amended. She wasn't going to depend on anyone to make her happy or be there for her or any of the other silly things that she often heard women moaning about when it came to their men.

She was in love? Well, fine. But she was damned if it was going to make a fool out of her.

Chapter 11

The man was obviously not cooperating

Charlie had awakened refreshed, revitalized, and ready for anything. It was seven-thirty exactly, but Lesley had already gone. She had planned to drop off the quote, to make certain that the job just completed came up to her usual standards, and to show him how in control she was.

Well, hell.

Walking up to the front porch she had an instant image of treading this same path Friday night. A flash of heat momentarily overwhelmed her, but she resisted the urge to fan herself. Reaching into her pocket, she pulled out the house key. Despite the urge she had to retain command of the small piece of metal, she planned to take it back to Mrs. C. as soon as she was done here today.

She took off her boots as soon as she entered the house. The place was quiet except for the ticking of the grandfather clock in the living room. The first thing she ought to do, she thought, forcing her mind back on track, was take a look in the attic. The sun was up and it was a brilliant day. Any flaws in the roofing would show themselves as tiny sunbeams dissecting the dark of that windowless space.

The stairs to the attic were on the second floor.

As she headed up, she wondered where she should leave the envelope with the bathroom estimate. Not in his bedroom. No, she really didn't want Lesley to know that she'd been drawn to go there. Of course, it occurred to her on Saturday afternoon that their activities the night before had done some damage to that beautiful old four-poster. She was handy with all things made of wood. It would only be fair for her to take a look, see what could be done to repair...

The four-poster was gone. In its place was another bed, this one with a brass headboard. It was a queen size and really took up a lot of space in the room. A frown marred her brow. Well, that was quick work. He must have gone out first thing Saturday morning to buy this and have it delivered Sunday. Of course, it was nothing to her. Maybe he was used to breaking beds and had the procedure for replacing them down pat. Maybe he kept a program for it on his computer, along with the telephone numbers and locations of furniture stores.

And maybe Chad is right and I am a complete moron.

With a low growl, she pivoted away from the bedroom—she'd begin to think of it as *the scene of the crime*—and headed toward the attic stairs. It was time for her to get to work and put away everything else that was cluttering up her brain.

She stopped when she passed another open door, then backtracked. There, in a heap in the middle of what appeared to be another bedroom, lay the carcass of the dead bed. Tied with a ribbon to one of the posts that was sticking into the air like a gravestone was a single red rose.

Drawn, Charlie entered the room. The rose was beautiful, just barely beginning to open, and long-stemmed. Perfume swirled around her like an erotic elixir devised to seduce. Taped to the stem was one of those tiny florist-shop cards. Printed neatly on it was her name and nothing more.

She didn't care if she did have a sappy grin on her face as she simply stood there and stroked the flower gently. No one had ever given her a rose before. She immediately forgave Lesley for not calling her all weekend. More, she admitted, but only to herself, that if anyone ought to have called with an apology, then *she* should have called *him*. The rose was beautiful, but she needed to remember to keep the upper hand in this situation.

Still, he'd given her a rose. The least she could do, after checking the attic for light leaks, was to see what she could do to fix the old bed. It was beautiful, made of solid oak. It had been built with care and had obviously been cherished through the years. She wondered if it was the bed that Lesley's Aunt and her husband had begun their married life with.

Imagine having only one bed for most of your adult life. One bed, one lover. Charlie blinked and shook her head, shivering. *Let's just ditch that sentiment right here and now.* Her self-admonition couldn't wipe the smile from her face. Turning away from the flower, she headed for the attic. First this inspection, then she'd see what she could do to give Lesley her own version of a thank-you-for-the-sex gesture.

* * * *

Lesley dropped his attaché case just inside the door and heaved a giant sigh of relief. Yanking loose his tie, he aimed his footsteps in the direction of the kitchen. First, a nice cold beer. Usually beer-after-work was a Friday treat, but this would make the second Monday in recent memory to share the honor. Of course, that other Monday had been more like a beer-after-coffee-after-incredibly-mind-blowing-life-altering-sex-after-work-day.

Lesley looked down to where his hopeful erection was trying to escape his pants.

"Down, fella. She's not here." But she had been. He knew that the moment he stepped into the kitchen and saw the white envelope on the kitchen table. He picked it up, beer forgotten, and resisted the urge to bring it to his face. Charlie didn't drench herself in artificial scent, so there would be no lingering aromatic impression on the paper. No, Charlie's scent was all woman. Clean, hot and carnal.

Well that image did nothing to discourage Lance down there, he thought as he shook his head. Then something occurred to him. Maybe she didn't get the gift he had left her.

It took him only moments to gain the second story. He stood, silly grin on his face, taking in the sight of the resurrected bed. The lack of a metal frame and box spring told him that Charlie hadn't repaired the thing the easy way. Curiosity had him scrunching down and peering underneath. She had replaced the broken timber with new and, he couldn't help but smile, what appeared to be stronger wood.

So, point one, his mind reasoned. She had been looking, so she'd not only found the rose—which was gone—but she had fixed the broken bed. She had been drawn to his bedroom, memories of Friday night and Saturday morning directing her feet, he would bet on it. Just as he could imagine her reaction when she looked in—probably had some smart-ass mental comment to seeing an entirely new bed in there. Had she taken a moment to ponder, as he had, the creative contributions that a brass headboard might make to an evening's entertainment? Perhaps not. He would be certain, at the very next opportunity, to expand her horizons in that regard. Point two: She had repaired the bed their lovemaking—not sex, but *lovemaking*—had broken. She'd felt responsible, and probably more than a little nostalgic, as the four-poster was made of very fine oak.

Smiling, he retreated to his downstairs office where he set the envelope on the desk, then turned on his computer. Deciding that the moment called for wine instead of beer, he went into the kitchen, poured himself a nice glass of zinfandel, then headed back to his office. For a long moment he sat and sipped, his mind considering the delightful puzzle that was Charlie McKinley as he read the quote she had left.

Then, plan set, he began to compose an e-mail.

* * * *

Charlie used soap-covered hands to sooth her strained muscles . She was tempted, but resisted the urge to have them relieve her of the arousal that had been humming through her system all afternoon. As she had worked on fixing that bed, first lugging the heavy lumber she'd had to purchase up the stairs, then working feverishly to finish the repair before five, scenes of Friday night had played on her mind like a continuous video feed. She could have sworn, as she bent over that old frame and worked that she could smell him, all clean and hot and male. Of course, that was just ridiculous. Further proof—as if she needed any—that the incredible mind-blowing sex had done just that…blown her mind.

As she rinsed and turned off the shower, Charlie found herself thinking that perhaps a working brain was overrated.

"Shit!" She really had to get a hold of herself. She dried off and tossed on her housecoat. Padding to her bedroom in bare feet, she shut the door behind her. She needed to get dressed, get down to her office, and finish the important work of submitting two bids for upcoming projects. It also wouldn't hurt, she thought, to have a look at the financial situation of her business. Taking those few days longer had nipped her profit margin on the Farmer job down to the bare bone. If he gave her the go-ahead on the bathroom, she hoped that he would want her to start soon.

She didn't know how she'd get through a day without some form of contact with Lesley, even if it was second hand contact through his house.

She pulled on blue jeans and a t-shirt, her gaze landing on the single red rose in a bud vase on her dresser. She was barely aware of the soft smile that kissed her lips. The next instant, her brow creased.

As for this 'love' business, she supposed she ought to give it some serious consideration. If he was in love with her—and she still wasn't one hundred percent convinced that he was—and if she was leaning in that same direction toward him, then she supposed that they should at least have some conversation on the matter.

Which probably meant, hell, she *would* have to apologize for stealing from his bed in the middle of the night like a thief. Charlie *hated* apologizing, absolutely hated it with every fiber of her being.

Heaving a sigh and giving the rose one light caress, she left her room and headed down. She swooped through the kitchen just long enough to grab a can of pasta in tomato sauce from the shelf, open it, shove a spoon in, and take a can of cola out of the fridge. Thus, armed with dinner, she retreated to her office.

She was in the middle of her first proposal when the little icon flashed on her computer, informing her that she had mail. She minimized the spreadsheet she had been working on, and then went to her on-line mailbox.

Her breathing hitched, her heart rate spiked and she felt herself get wet. Hell of a reaction to seeing a man's name in the "sender" column. Calling herself an idiot, since he was likely just responding to the quote she'd left him, she clicked the read option.

Charlie,

Your generous offer is simply irresistible. As I've already had the pleasure to discover, the work of your hands is breathtaking, your attention to detail nearly mind-shattering. As I sit here, all alone on this quiet evening, there is no one else I can picture in my shower…on my bathroom floor…working on my pipes…except you. I am a lucky man to have such a wonderful laborer as you are, seeing so satisfyingly to my needs.

I'm ready for you to begin again, the sooner the better.

I'd also like to thank you. You, and only you, brought life back to that old four-poster bed. I know it wasn't easy, and I don't want you to think that your sacrifice of time and effort has gone unappreciated. I have a very soft spot in my heart for, and extremely fond memories of, that particular piece of furniture.

Looking forward to continuing our…association.

Lesley

Charlie grabbed the stack of envelopes that sat by her printer and fanned herself quickly. She wanted him. In fact, she had a good mind to just go over there right now and jump his damned bones. The tease! Was there anything more sneaky than sending an innuendo-laced e-mail to accept a job quote from a woman you just happened to have laid a few times?

Well, yeah, there was, she admitted in the next instant. Creeping from the man's bed just shy of dawn had been pretty damn sneaky.

She understood why she had done it, of course. The emotions Lesley Farmer stirred in her had flooded her, taken over her body and her mind and her soul until she was afraid, very much afraid, that she would somehow lose herself completely.

Chad had been absolutely right about her. She did need to feel in control. She always had, though she'd never admitted it to herself before, nor given it a great deal of thought.

Was he right about the rest of it? If she continued to run, to shy away from these feelings, would she one day be as broken-hearted as he was? Was it a theory she really cared to test?

Or did she want to see where all this was leading? Did she really have the courage for that? Then, more honestly—and more to the point—she asked herself if she really had a choice.

As much as a part of her longed to get in her truck, take a short drive, and fuck a certain librarian's brains out, she wasn't going to. She had a feeling he might be expecting her to do just that, and *damned* if she was going to be predictable. Not allowing herself another moment to think, worry or ponder, she clicked the 'reply' button on the e-mail document. The words came fast and without much thought.

No, the thinking part came just before she hit "send." She programmed the computer to send her response to Lesley at eight-fifteen tomorrow morning.

It was nearly ten p.m. now. She reasoned that if he was going to mess with her getting a good night's sleep, the least she could do in return was to spice up his Tuesday.

Chapter 12

Lesley was nearly late for work and it was all her fault.

After sending that e-mail—and knowing that she'd read it as he had put a check mark in that nifty little "notify me when this e-mail has been read" box—he half expected her to storm his ramparts. In fact, he'd been looking forward to it. He had it all planned out. He would let her rant and rave or whatever other activity she had in mind as he walked her up to his bedroom. Then he'd let her vent her frustrations out on him in a more hands-on, personal way.

She hadn't come over, of course, and Lesley knew that he really couldn't blame Charlie for his sleepless night. That bit of silliness meant to torment her had ricocheted right back at him. He had dreamt of her last night in sharp, erotic detail. His dreams hadn't been satisfied to replay everything they'd done together, either. Oh, no, they had to give him a preview of all the things he'd been thinking of doing with her, too.

Lesley was amazed how much heavier the traffic was fifteen minutes later than he normally traveled. By the time he arrived on campus and parked in his designated spot near the library complex, he was ready for a break. But, of course, this being the first Tuesday of a new month, and therefore a seminar morning, there was no break in sight.

The meeting ended at eleven, and in an act of professional cowardice he turned the guest speaker over to Melissa for her to fawn over and pamper.

A couple of members of his staff needed his advice on matters relating to their specific duties, and so it was a quarter to twelve before he was finally able to sequester himself in his office. Logging on to his computer, he had only one goal in mind. He deserved a few minutes of down time. Accessing his personal e-mail, he grinned when he saw one message in particular. He wondered what Charlie would have to say about his 'acceptance' of her quote.

Lesley,

Thank you for the opportunity to continue serving you. As I read your acceptance, I very nearly came right then and there! But then I knew it would be better, much better, to wait for a new day when I could be rested, ready and raring to go.

I'm looking forward to spending time in your shower. You have my personal guarantee that my attention to detail will be absolute. When I'm done, you'll be hotter, and wetter, than ever before.

I will, of course, pay very close attention to your pipes, my hands firm but gentle as I ensure that all is in proper working order. No matter how long, or how hard, I will not rest until I'm completely done.

You have my word that at the end of the day, you will be very, very satisfied with my work. Charlie

"Have mercy," Lesley hissed through his teeth as he read through the correspondence a second time. He was willing to surrender right on the spot. Had he ever thought Charlie less than his match, intellectually? What an idiot he'd been!

What an idiot he was now, sitting in his office with his penis at attention and no Charlie in sight.

Then he remembered it was lunchtime.

Disengaging the computer and jumping to his feet, he winced as it registered that moving in a full state of arousal was not only painful, but potentially embarrassing too. A sweater hung on the coat tree in the corner of his office. He snatched it, folded it over his arm, and, carrying it in front of him, headed out.

Luck was with him as he made it from the building to his car without being seen. He drove more quickly than the law allowed. Getting a speeding ticket would be a fair price to pay, under the circumstances. It was lunchtime and he was *very* hungry. There was only one thing that would satisfy this hunger, and if Fate smiled on him, she'd still be at his place.

He felt downright predatory as he swung his car to the curb in front of his house. His eyes narrowed at the pick-up that was in his drive. He checked his watch: 12:05. Taking the porch steps two at a time, he was at the door in thirty seconds. His nose scented the air as a wild creature scents out his mate. Voices hummed in the background. He was nearly at the top of the stairs when he realized that it was two voices he could hear. Charlie, and someone else. Some *male* someone else. His brain nearly fumbled the ball. Just before he reached the bathroom, he remembered that Charlie had a kid working with her—Timmy or Tommy or something.

"Hi Dr. Farmer!"

Lesley barely gave a nod, acknowledging the young man's greeting. His eyes were all on Charlie. And while the kid seemed to be deaf and dumb to the hormonal vibes exploding like fireworks all around them, Charlie wasn't.

"Ah...Tom...why don't you take my truck and go get those materials we just listed? And grab yourself some lunch while you're at it. I...I completely forgot that Dr. Farmer was wanting to meet with me for a few minutes..."

"Probably an hour, at least, Ms. McKinley."

"Right," Charlie corrected, licking her lips. "Probably an hour at least. Here," she held out her keys.

Tom took the keys. "Sure, I can do that. Likely by the time Virgil down at the building supply store gets me loaded up and then I have lunch...probably be closer to two hours before I get back."

"Good man," Lesley breathed.

Neither of them moved for several moments after Tom left the house.

"Charlie."

"Yes, Lesley?"

He reached for her hand and, walking backwards, led her out of the bathroom and down the hall into his bedroom.

"Kid's smarter than he looks. We've got two hours."

"I should probably be pissed about the way you just did that."

"I should probably be pissed about the way you snuck from my bed Saturday morning as if you were ashamed to be there."

"No! God, no, it wasn't that! It was…"

"I know what it was, Charlie." His voice softer, he pulled her closer, kissed her nose, then began to get her out of her clothes. "The dates didn't work out, but that doesn't seem to matter. It appears that we're smack dab in the middle of a relationship anyway. Agreed?"

He paused in the act of unbuttoning her shirt and waited.

"Agreed. We…ah, we should probably discuss ground rules, or something."

"Good idea. Here's the first one: the next time you find yourself in my bed for the night, no leaving before breakfast."

He kept his hands still on her clothing, and when she finally looked up into his eyes he knew by her expression that she realized how serious he was.

"No leaving before breakfast," she echoed in a bare whisper.

Before she could say another word his lips captured hers in a kiss that was wet and wild and carnal. His hands resumed stripping her, feverishly. Still deep into the lip lock, his fingers combed through the hair on her mound and then plunged. He caught her weight as her knees buckled and her body shivered. Lifting her, he walked backwards toward the bed even as he unbuckled his belt, opened his trousers and let them drop to the floor. Sitting on the edge of the bed he rolled on a condom then brought her down onto his lap, impaling her in one sure stroke.

Both hands clamped low on her hips, he urged her to ride.

She whimpered and he smiled.

"Me too," he whispered, his mouth fastening on hers again. "Give me everything, Charlie."

"Come inside me. I want to feel you come inside me."

Lesley knew he was mere seconds from doing just that. Reaching down between them, he moistened his fingers in their wetness and began to stroke and tease her clitoris.

He relished the sound of her scream as her orgasm crashed through her, as she absorbed the spasms of his ejaculation. Breathing hard, they rested for a moment, forehead against forehead.

"I have tickets to the game tomorrow night," Lesley said, his hands stroking up and down her back. "Want to come with me?"

"I think I just did," she whispered, earning a playful swat.

"Minx. I'm asking you out on a date. One that I think will go much better than the other two we attempted."

"I love basketball."

"Me too."

"I hated that weight lifting competition."

"Ditto. And everything you said about that stuff at the gallery was exactly the way I felt. I just made the mistake of taking your words personally."

"We've made a lot of mistakes, the two of us. Maybe we can change that."

"I'd like to. I want to have more than just sex with you, although the sex is pretty damn spectacular."

"Yeah, it is, isn't it?" As if to underline her agreement, she moved her hips slowly back and forth. He was still inside her, and hardening again. "Any idea how much of that two hours we've already used?"

He took a quick check of his watch. "Yeah. About fifteen minutes."

"Heaven help us," she whispered as she captured his mouth.

Lesley grunted, then kicked out of his shoes and pants. Thirty seconds later his shirt was history, and he'd lifted Charlie and brought her down on his bed.

"Another hour or so of this might just kill us."

"I'm a brave woman. I'll risk it."

* * * *

It was exactly ten-thirty the next morning, and Charlie stood silently just outside Lesley's office. Noting that there was a young woman sitting across from him, she cleared her throat to announce her presence.

Lesley seemed to understand exactly why she was there. It had occurred to her, just this very morning, that as wonderful as yesterday had been, it wouldn't do to let Dr. Farmer think he could barge in and disrupt her day and get away with it. How did that help her keep the upper hand in this relationship thing?

"I'm sorry. Am I early?"

"Charlie."

"Because I do recall that yesterday you told me to come."

"Ah…Melissa."

"Hi Melissa, I'm Charlie. I'm working on Dr. Farmer's house, and we have an urgent matter to discuss."

"Well, it *is* break time," Melissa said.

"Thank you, Melissa. I'll…I'll let you know when I'm free."

Charlie closed the door behind the departing Melissa, and turned the lock. Then she faced Lesley and fairly stalked him.

"This is a nice surprise." He had apparently recovered from his shock at seeing her at his office door. She was intent on seeing him shocked speechless.

"No, this is equal measure."

She walked around his desk, and he instinctively swiveled his chair to face her. Her grip was strong as she yanked him to his feet.

Before he could say a word she had his belt unfastened and his pants opened.

"Melissa better figure out that you're not free. I don't share."

"Melissa? No, I didn't mean...we don't...that is to say...." He let out a huff of breath as Charlie shoved him back into his chair. In the next instant she was on her knees in front of him.

"Glad we got that settled. I guess that's ground rule number two. No sharing. Now, what time were you going to pick me up for the game tonight?"

"Well, I thought...."

Words strangled off as Charlie took his cock into her mouth and proceeded to suck every thought right out of his head.

Chapter 13

"Get a clue, Ref! That was a foul!"

Lesley chuckled as Charlie plopped back down in the seat next to him, nodding her head in satisfaction at having bellowed her opinion.

"Bloody ref is biased, I tell you," she continued, just slightly less loudly, to him. "That foul couldn't have been more blatant."

"No argument here. So, you ever play?"

"Yeah, some." Without taking her eyes from the action on the court, she was able to reach with unerring accuracy into the popcorn container that Lesley was holding on his lap. "Mostly just, you know, pick up games with my brothers."

"Didn't join the team in high school? I'd have thought that with your love of the game you would have."

Charlie didn't answer right away, and when the ref blew his whistle, Lesley looked over at her. She was blushing.

"You don't have to be embarrassed if you weren't good enough to make the team, Charlie."

"I was good enough," she said, the defiance of a teenager glinting in her eyes and edging her words. When Lesley didn't take the bait, simply sat and waited, she ducked her head. "Made the team. Got booted off." She looked at him then. "One of the most common notes in my school file was 'doesn't play well with others.'"

"I didn't, either. Play well with others. Being around the other kids intimidated the hell out of me. I was a scrawny nerd who was much more comfortable on his own."

"Yeah, well, according to some of my teachers, I was the one guilty of doing the intimidating. Wouldn't have happened if people did things the right way in the first damn place."

"I find it awfully hard to believe that anyone would claim you were intimidating."

Charlie's mouth twitched in a smile. Punching him lightly in the arm, she said, "That wasn't nice."

The play had resumed, and both sets of eyes were on the game.

"So tell me something about you I don't know."

"Okay. I have *two* Margaret Lynwood Sawyers in my attic."

"You're kidding me!" He took his eyes off the action on the court and focused on Charlie's face.

"Nope. No kidding."

"With the one you made me pay five hundred bucks for, I have three. Between us, we have a quarter of the entire collection!"

"I didn't make you pay five hundred for it. You could have let me buy it at any time."

"Funny lady."

Charlie jumped to her feet, joining half the spectators in her coaching. "Shoot it! Shoot!"

The crowd roared their approval as the player obviously listened and scored three points.

Lesley moved quickly, swooping in and stealing a kiss. "How in hell did I ever enjoy watching a game without you?"

"Beats weightlifting, huh?"

"All to hell."

* * * *

The renovations were coming along much faster than he imagined they would. The next morning, as Lesley looked at the progress of the upstairs bath on his way back up from the downstairs one, he realized he had a potential problem.

He couldn't think of any way to guarantee himself access to Charlie until he won her mind and heart as well as her body *except* that he keep her working on his house. He knew she was commitment shy, but he hadn't realized until last night that the problem was more complex than that. At the game he had learned something about her that he bet was one of her core traits: she needed to feel in control. All the time.

He had to keep her around until he could prove to her that commitment did not equal powerlessness.

As he dressed for the day, he considered the situation. The truth of the matter was, when he inherited this house, he had planned to renovate it. It came as no surprise to him that the roof needed to be replaced or the plumbing updated. The house was a relatively small structure on a large piece of land. It was a fine size for him now, but if he planned to marry and have a family, the house would need to be bigger. He envisioned a two-story addition on the back, off the kitchen, to make it into the home he would eventually need. The home he wanted to share with Charlie.

Of course, he couldn't tell her that. A mischievous grin lit his face. Perhaps he could let her think he was planning to improve the condition of the place to put it on the market.

Lesley didn't feel the least bit guilty as he decided on his plan. He had finally found the woman he wanted to spend the rest of his life with. She was being particularly thick about things at the moment, but there was no doubt in his mind that she would come to see that they were meant for each other. He had no doubt that eventually she would come to the conclusion that a life with him was simply irresistible.

It was just going to take planning, and time.

* * * *

Charlie stepped back from her work and stretched the kinks out of her back. As soon as Tom returned, they'd begin to install the vanity countertop and sink. When her cell phone rang, her eyes continued to examine the work she'd just completed as she pulled the phone out of her back pocket.

A quick check of the call display showed an already familiar number and put a smile on her face.

"Dr. Farmer's residence. The doc can't come to the phone right now. I have him handcuffed and gagged, naked, on his bed. Can I take a message?"

"You want me to come home for lunch again?" Lesley asked, a chuckle in his voice.

"Well that would be nice. Tuesday's lunch was certainly memorable."

"Yes, it was. And there's nothing I'd like more. Unfortunately, I'm having regurgitated budget for lunch. What are you having?"

"Oh, yuck, there's an image. I hadn't actually realized it was lunchtime. I think I have a can of Spam and some bread in my lunch bucket. Might have forgotten my mustard, though. Okay if I use yours?" She leaned back against the wall, relaxing into the conversation.

"More than okay. Use anything you want, Charlie. Spam and bread, is it? Not sure I've ever tried that particular culinary combination."

"You don't know what you're missing."

"I'll take your word for it. So, do you have anything planned for tonight?"

"Yeah. I promised an older couple, friends of my folks, that I'd come by for dinner and have a look at some work they need done to their house. Then tomorrow, M.E. and I are going to a movie. We try to do that at least a couple Fridays a month."

"Busy lady. If you're not already all booked up for Saturday, why not come over? Sometime in the afternoon would be good. I'll make dinner."

"You cook?" The prospect of a Saturday night being fed by Lesley put a smile on her face.

"I like to eat, so yeah, I cook."

"Hey, I like to eat too, but I *hate* cooking." And had, ever since her brothers had tried to manipulate her into being *their* full-time cook.

"Well, I enjoy it."

"Can I bring anything? Like, dessert?"

"You just said you don't cook."

"They have bakeries now. They're everywhere."

"Smart ass. Just bring a couple of DVDs. And your toothbrush."

His voice had taken on that deep soft tone that made her insides melt. "Not my jammies?" she asked.

"You could bring them, if you like," he replied, "but I'm only going to take them off you."

"You're pretty cocky."

"Ah, I hate to brag. Glad you noticed."

Her insides had gone from melting to molten. She heard the catch in her own voice and hoped that sound affected him. "Like I could miss."

"Well, you had me handcuffed and gagged, naked on the bed at the beginning of this conversation. Can't blame a man for getting ideas."

"I'll be gentle. I promise."

"You don't have to be gentle, baby. You just have to be relentless."

"You're expecting me to get right back to work after that?" She almost wanted to rub her legs together to stem the moisture.

"No, Charlie. Have lunch first. Then get back to work. I have to finish this budget surgery and then attend a meeting in the Chancellor's office."

"I think I'm getting the better deal, here."

"I know you are. Take care."

"You too."

* * * *

Saturday dawned bright and sunny and the forecast was for a nice warm day. Lesley left the house just after nine, his list of errands engraved on his mind.

His last stop was an adult novelty store.

That brass headboard was just begging for a pair of restraints. The idea had flitted across his mind when he'd moved that bed into his room. But since his lunchtime conversation with Charlie on Thursday, the image simply hadn't gone away.

He took longer than he'd planned to in the store. He never knew that there were so many different accessories available for couples to enhance their lovemaking. He found himself considering more than just the steel handcuffs. There were potions and lotions that raised his eyebrow and his sap. He thought the massage oil and personal lubricant might be interesting, especially since it boasted of "tingling" properties. He gave a pass on the edible underwear, and could only stare in wonder at some of the other toys offered in the specialty store. Next time, he promised himself, he'd bring Charlie with him. There was, he decided, a whole world out there just waiting to be explored.

He arrived home just before noon. Slicing the pork and vegetables so they'd be ready to cook, he set them in the fridge. Next, smiling all the way, he headed upstairs, changed the sheets on the bed, and set out a few candles. The handcuffs he wound around a center rail on the headboard. Just above them, within easy reach, he taped a hook, and slipped the key onto it. He had once heard a horror story about a man and woman who had been engaged in recreational sex, and the man had died of a heart attack, leaving his lover handcuffed to the bed, days passing before she was found.

Not that Lesley planned on having any coronary episodes, but being anal, and having heard that story, he took the precaution.

He stood back and smiled. The handcuffs weren't visible. They would be his little after dinner surprise.

* * * *

"I thought you weren't going to bring any pajamas," Lesley said as he opened the door to Charlie a couple hours later.

"I didn't."

He kept his eyes on the black knapsack she had slung over her shoulder and gulped comically. "Should I be worried?"

"Only if you were planning a *really* late breakfast tomorrow. I have an every-Sunday-morning-at-ten squash date with M.E."

"You do?"

"What's that smile about?"

"I have an every-Sunday-afternoon-at-one squash date with Percy."

"Let me guess: you play squash at the UnClub?"

"See? We have a lot of things in common. Sex. Art. Sex. Entertainment. Sex. Sports. Sex."

"Especially the sex," she said, moving in fast and locking her lips on his as if there was to be no letting go. Lesley wasted no time in hauling her close and joining her in the mutual plunder.

"I love the taste of you, Charlie. Here," he licked her lips, then moved on, laved her neck, "and here. Here," her shoulder. "So many different and delicious flavors."

"Me, too. I think I might be getting addicted to you."

"I like the sound of that."

"You would."

The words sounded half teasing, half worried, so he gathered her into a tight hug.

"This particular addiction won't harm you, honey. I promise."

"That's not how it feels."

Lesley was grinning because she sounded so forlorn, and because she was broaching a topic he'd not known how to. Rubbing his hands up and down her back, he murmured, "I know. But maybe it will feel less threatening, in time."

Charlie stepped out of his embrace, then placed a quick kiss on his lips.

"I don't know why it is, though I've been trying to figure it out just lately. Maybe it comes from being the youngest in the family. It's been kind of a running joke in my family for years—Charlie has to be in control of everything all the time. But it's not funny. Not in this instance."

"No, it's not."

"And I do feel out of control where you're concerned."

"I know you do, Charlie. But you're not. Nothing happens against your will. I'll never tell you what to do. Not ever."

"Uh huh."

"I may suggest, strongly," he conceded, grinning. "But that's as far as it goes. Besides," he took a moment to test her biceps, "I think you're stronger than me."

"Damn right I am. I can kick your ass any time I have a mind to."

"I'm scared."

"Good. After I drop my bag upstairs, what do you want to do?"

"I've got wine, and I've got beer. Take your pick. I thought we'd just sit together and chat for a while. Both of us have had busy weeks. I need some down time, and I want it to be with you."

"Sounds like a plan."

Chapter 14

"Your parents weren't very nice to you."

"You make it sound as if I was an abused kid, and I wasn't, Charlie. They had different priorities, and different ideas on how to raise a son. Their summers were for archeological digs. So they brought me here where I got to be a kid."

The afternoon was slowly creeping toward evening. They were stretched out on a chaise in the back yard, sipping wine and simply talking. However their relationship had begun, it seemed now that they both wanted to cover the steps that they'd skipped in the beginning.

"Growing up in my house was noisy. There were always lots of fights and hugs and love. We didn't have fancy vacations anywhere. But each summer, there were day trips to the beach and of course, we went to the Canadian National Exhibition every year."

"Sounds like fun."

"It was."

"How'd you get into construction?"

"Mom says it's Dad's fault," she answered, laughing softly. "Dad's hobby is woodworking. Right from the time I was little I knew it was what I loved. I decided that I didn't want college. Mom's still a bit ticked about that. Instead, I got a job on a construction site. And went from there, to working on my own."

"You aiming to have a big company some day?"

"You mean like…job sites from here to there and slinging up commercial high-rises? No. It's not about the money – beyond having enough to live on. It's about the work. I love the work."

* * * *

"When I inherited this house, I had plans. Things that I knew needed fixing or replacing."

They had left the back yard and were in the kitchen. Charlie hadn't bothered to ask if she could help him with the dinner preparations. She had already told him she hated to cook.

"I hadn't really put a timetable on getting the work done," Lesley continued, "but I had a list. Replacing the roof was actually number one, and refurbishing the bathroom upstairs was on it, too. But the major thing I wanted to see done was to have a two story addition put on out the back."

"How big of an addition?" Charlie asked as she wandered to the open screen door and looked out on the back yard.

"I was thinking two really good sized rooms down—with a central hallway leading to a door outside, and two big bedrooms upstairs."

"Balcony on the upstairs bedrooms, overlooking the yard? You'd have a view of the park and the river beyond, I think. It would be a nice feature. Balconies are big these days."

"That sounds good. And maybe one of the downstairs rooms should be like...oh, I don't know, a granny suite?"

"That would be smart, Lesley. More and more families are staying together longer, or taking in elderly parents." It would be smart. But there was a niggling voice in the back of her mind. She had replaced his roof and was working on his upstairs bathroom. Now, just as that job was finishing up, he was talking about even more renovations. Not that she minded. She loved what she did and did it well. But she wanted to earn jobs on the merit of her building skills, and nothing more. "Is it because you want to give me work?" She asked at last.

Lesley looked over his shoulder at her and shook his head.

"In my office, in the file cabinet, top drawer. The folder marked 'house.' Go ahead and take a look."

Charlie only needed a moment to decide she wanted to assuage her curiosity. Following Lesley's directions, she pulled the appropriate folder from his file cabinet. Looking around, she thought his home office *was* awfully small. She brought the file back to the kitchen. Pulling out a chair, she sat at the table and began going through the surprisingly thick folder. The list he'd referred to was about midway through it, and she smiled as she read it. The last item on the list was 'revised evaluation: resale value'.

Charlie guessed it made perfect sense for Lesley to want to fix up the place and put it on the market.

"I'm not playing 'make work for my woman' here, Charlie. But the truth is, if the work is going to be done on this place anyway, why shouldn't it be you doing it? I'm more than happy with what you've done so far, and, most importantly, I trust you."

"That's...that's nice. I got a nice little warm gush inside when you said that. Thanks."

"You're welcome. So, what do you think?"

"I know an architect who could use the work. He's just starting out but he's good. I could do the plans myself, but I think you deserve to have them professionally made. He's not very expensive. I could set up a meeting."

"Please. Now, enough shop talk. Dinner will be ready in a few minutes."

"Huh. It doesn't look like you've slaved over a hot stove all day."

"Naw, not all day. Just a half hour. You may discover, my dear, that the best things in life are simpler than you could possibly imagine."

"You're putting your cooking skills right up there with the best things in life, are you?"

"I never claimed to be modest."

* * * *

"You going to get a dishwasher?"

"Maybe, some day. I kind of like washing dishes by hand. Good thinking time."

"Oh yeah? What have you been thinking about?" Charlie had picked up the tea towel when Lesley put the dishes in to soak. They'd been working well together on the mundane chore.

One thing he was right about, she mused. His cooking should be considered one of the best things in life.

"Dessert."

"Dessert? How can you think about food after that meal? Which was wonderful, by the way."

"Thank you."

"You're welcome. What's for dessert?"

Lesley walked over to her and slowly pulled her into his arms. "Guess."

She felt as if her bones were melting. He had this affect on her every single time. It was part of that not-being-in-control thing that she hated, but right at this moment, as his tongue swirled and dipped and danced with her own, as his hands slid so silkily down her back to her bottom, it was hard to remember why that should bother her.

He was hard. Her hips convulsed against his erection. As she had once before, she climbed him, her arms wrapping around his neck and her legs around his hips.

She trusted him not to drop her, she realized in one hazy moment, and then stopped thinking altogether.

"I want you in my bed," he hissed. One hand was at the back of her head, the other on her ass, squeezing even as he supported her.

"Too far away." Her hands were busy seeking buttons to open on his shirt.

"Minx. I've been dreaming of having you there all week."

Charlie was impressed that he was able to carry her up the stairs. She was perplexed when he managed to set her on her feet. She was about to say something acerbic about the meaning of the term 'getting laid,' but then he was moving away from her, lighting candles.

"Romance?"

"Screw romance. I want to see you naked, by candlelight."

Charlie's eruption of laughter was cut short as Lesley frantically whipped her shirt over her head, opened and discarded her bra and had his hands on her naked breasts in ten seconds flat. Gasping, she could do nothing but bow back as he replaced his hands with his mouth, as his tongue and teeth teased and tormented first one nipple, then the other.

She helped him out of his shirt, and then turned her attention to his pants. He took over the task, shucking the last of his clothes with careless disregard for the material.

When he lifted her and slid her pants and panties from her, she kicked free of them and wrapped her legs around him once more. That first contact of his engorged penis against her pussy brought them both to the point of groaning. Absorbing the coolness of the sheets against her hot flesh, Charlie closed her eyes and savored the weight of Lesley's body. All firm muscle, he pressed her deeper into the bed. She sighed as he claimed her mouth once more, his hands smoothing down her arms, his fingers linking with hers.

His tongue and lips lapped and suckled and Charlie was lost in the taste of him as she was consumed by the never-sated craving for him. He stretched her arms above her head, and she could only respond by arching her back and offering him more. She only wanted to give, to feed the fire that was burning so hotly between them. She lifted her hips, caressing his cock within the folds of her labia, and then she went shock still as cold metal snapped around her wrists.

"What..."

"Shhh...just let me love you, Charlie. Let me claim every inch of you, let me have you completely."

"Lesley."

"Yes, baby, I feel it too."

He raised his head, his gaze connecting with hers.

"What the hell is this?" A sharp tug on the handcuffs punctuated her question.

"I can't give you complete credit for the idea. The thought crossed my mind the morning I moved this bed over..."

"No, my idea, as I recall, was you wearing the hardware."

"Look up."

She did, and it took her a moment to see there was a key dangling very close to her hands. It was close enough that she knew she could reach it.

"You can take them off if you want to. If you need to. Or you can know that I won't hurt you, and continue with this fantasy. You can trust me enough to let go, just for a little while. I'll understand if you choose not to. I'll understand and be okay with it. But I'm hoping you'll choose to trust me."

He was asking for her trust. She could no longer claim that they barely knew each other; they knew each other very well. She could no longer claim not to know what was happening between them. She was falling in love with him. He'd already told her, in his way, that he felt the same way about her.

The look in his eyes told her that he was reading her thoughts right now.

She hated that she wanted to grab that key and unlock the manacles. She hated that it was her first instinct, to escape and to be self-sufficient. Self-serving. Alone.

It was her choice, completely. She knew him well enough to know that was a fact.

"Kiss me." She wished the words had emerged stronger, the demand a woman of strength could make on her lover.

"Where?" He began light butterfly caresses on her eyes, her cheeks. "Here?" He licked the corner of her mouth and then his lips possessed hers in a blatantly carnal assault. "Or there? Or maybe here." He sipped and licked his way to her breasts, where he suckled strongly on each nipple in turn, making her hips convulse in response. He stroked one hand down, petting her pussy in sync with his sucking, so that she was rocking with a rhythm that was slow, steady and demanding.

"Mmm, nice, you like this. But I did mention dessert, didn't I?"

Slithering down her body he replaced his fingers with his mouth, his lips and tongue tasting, teasing and tantalizing.

Charlie cried out as the steel around her wrists was forgotten, as the liquid fire of his tongue stroking her clit ignited flames within her. She pushed her mound in his face, writhing as her arousal climbed high and fast, racing her heart and stealing her breath. She had one clear moment to wonder how she could be so hot, so horny without exploding. Then she felt Lesley slide his fingers inside her, and she came in a burst of shivering, throbbing, sobbing fireworks. Before she could draw a breath, before her last scream of pleasure died, he'd surged up and into her, his cock hitting hard and deep. She didn't understand that he had set her hands free, she only knew that she could wrap her self around him, arms and legs, as she needed to, holding on to ride the second wave of orgasm that crashed through her. His mouth devoured hers. She could taste herself on his lips and tongue and beyond all reason she came harder.

For long seconds there was nothing but the sound of two people gasping for breath.

"I'm wrecked. I'll get off you in a minute. As soon as I know if I'm still alive."

"Me too. And I think you must be, because I can feel your cock giving little shivers of delight inside me."

"Could be death throes."

"I hope not."

"Yeah. I didn't mean to make you feel threatened, Charlie."

"I know. I think I might have been okay with it if we had discussed it first."

"My fault. I guess I thought we had. Your trusting me was a wonderful gift, sweetheart. Thank you."

With a soft brush of fingers she caressed his face. Finding no words to say, she reached up and kissed him lightly.

Content for the moment, she snuggled more deeply into him and fell asleep.

Chapter 15

His cock was in her wet, wonderful mouth.

Not quite awake, he groaned, surged his hips, and followed his instincts to thread his fingers through her hair.

His wrists were encased in steel.

"My fantasy, my turn."

The feel of the words vibrated against his penis adding to already unbelievable pleasure. His blood heated and shivers raced up and down his spine. The slide of her tongue, the gentle suction of her lips was the most wonderful thing he'd ever felt.

"By all means," he said, his words breath-bare.

Helpless to do anything else, he lay back and enjoyed. Better than his most erotic wet dream, he longed to prolong the experience. He thought if he could wrap his mind around some sort of complex philosophical debate, maybe he could keep himself from... At that moment her hand wandered down to caress his balls, and he was lost. The orgasm ripped through him, more electric than anything he'd ever experienced because she was sucking the semen right out of him. He was left a quivering and quaking mass, and totally empty.

Charlie moaned and kept up her attentions.

"Ah...sweetheart?" How could she not have noticed that she'd been successful? He'd just come in her mouth!

"You told me I had to be relentless. So I am."

"Oh God."

Her low sexy laughter helped to arouse him for a second time. He wondered if he could rise to the occasion for an encore. He'd hate to think she was expending herself in vain. Fortunately, before long, he was hard again.

Letting go of him with a loud slurp, she crawled up his body. Reaching into the bedside table drawer, she pulled out a condom and did a rather spectacular job of slowly rolling it in place. Then she impaled herself on his revitalized cock. Slowly, rhythmically, she rode him until he was almost begging for mercy. It felt so good to be inside her. The friction of his penis created little shivers in her that in turn caressed his length. The little noises that erupted from her throat turned him on even more, fed a machismo within him that he hadn't known was there. She arched and cried out, and the rippling of the orgasm along her vaginal walls triggered his.

She collapsed on him, laboring for breath, exhausted. After a moment she slid to his side, snuggling close.

When his heart rate settled some, he kissed the top of her head. "You going to unlock these?" He rattled the steel so she'd know what he meant.

"Mmm. In a minute."

Lesley looked up, but the key wasn't there. Turning his head to the side, he saw it glistening in the moonlight, just out of reach, on the bedside table where he'd left it earlier.

"Charlie?"

A soft snore was his only response. Too exhausted and satisfied to care, he closed his eyes. He might wake up in the morning with sore arms, but all things considered, that wasn't such a hefty price to pay.

* * * *

"Let me massage your shoulders some more."

"Sweetheart, you're going to be late. I don't want your best friend to hate me before she even meets me."

"I'll call her and cancel. She'll understand."

"I'm fine. Hey…." Lesley used a finger to tilt her chin up so she could see his eyes. "I was a little sore when I lowered my arms first thing this morning. But the hot shower—and you—took care of that."

"I feel so bad. I can't believe I left you like that all night. You should have woke me up."

"I don't feel so bad. That was the best night of my life."

"I'm sorry." Charlie wound her arms around his neck and hugged him tightly.

"You're sorry that you gave me the best night of my life?"

"No, I'm sorry I left you handcuffed to the headboard all night."

"It was just one of those everyday household accidents. It could have happened to anyone."

Charlie's shoulders shook with laughter. She knew that was exactly what Lesley had been aiming for when he gave her an extra hard squeeze before setting her back slightly.

"Truth is, it was my fault the key wasn't where it should have been. And considering how quickly I fell asleep after you had your way with me, it was fine. Stop beating yourself up over it. Go on now, or Megan Elizabeth is going to be pissed."

Charlie wondered how many other men would be as understanding as Lesley was. When she'd opened her eyes this morning and looked up, she thought her heart was going to stop. And while he'd groaned as she helped him lower his arms, he hadn't said a cross word or given her hell at all.

"Okay, I'll go. But I'll call you later this afternoon."

"That would be nice. Or, even better, you could come back. I should be home myself by four."

His suggestion had been softly spoken, with just the right amount of boyish hopefulness that she had to smile. She had never stayed over two nights in a row with a lover. That fact occurred to her as she found herself giving him a slight smile.

"Yeah, maybe I could do that."

* * * *

"Girlfriend, you are hot today!"

"Everything seems to be working well for me. I feel nice and loose."

"Must have been a good evening."

"Oh yeah," she laughed, giving up any pretence of propriety and waving her hand in short little swivels. Megan Elizabeth cackled, and they both sat down for a moment to take a breather.

"You want to play another set? We have the court for another twenty minutes."

Charlie smiled as her friend hammed it up, as if she was deeply torn.

"Well, I'd rather hear about your hot date last night," Megan said, smiling as she spoke. "Seeing as how I am currently getting my thrills vicariously through you."

"It was…I don't know how to describe it. We were in the back yard, snuggled on a chaise and just sipping wine and talking. A bit about our weeks, and some family stuff. And it felt…." Charlie was aware that there was a dreamy smile on her face. She didn't care.

"Homey."

"Yeah. Homey." She felt her smile slip, and wondered why.

"Uh oh. Charlie's commitment alarm just went off."

"No, there's no commitment. Well, other than the basic no bouncing on anyone else while you're bouncing on me rule."

"Uh huh. So then what happened?"

"Oh, he made dinner and then we…well, we never did get around to watching those DVDs I took. Maybe tonight."

"You're going back there tonight?"

"Actually later this afternoon. Around four." Charlie felt herself getting defensive. She got up from the bench and scooped up her sports bag.

"And you're going to talk about your day while he makes dinner. Again."

The dryness in her friend's tone stopped her. "Okay, I'm obviously missing something here. You were the one who urged me to talk to the guy, to grovel and apologize for being an idiot and give this...relationship...a chance. Now you're, like, a really ominous Greek Chorus of one. What gives?"

"I'm your best friend. I thought this entire thing began on the wrong foot, and I was just cheering you on when you so obviously wanted me to." Megan stopped speaking long enough to pick up her own racket bag. "But now it seems as if this relationship—and if you will note you had to pause before you said that word—is turning serious. I'm worried that you'll get in too deep before you realize it."

"I'm in love with him. Is that deep enough for you?" Charlie hadn't meant to say it out loud, as if it was a done deal. And she could tell by the look on Megan's face that she had truly shocked her friend.

"Well."

"You could say something more than that, like 'congratulations' or 'finally,' since this is a first for me. Feel free, even, to make a smart ass crack. You're really good at those."

"I would, if you were smiling and soppy and grinning like a puppy when you said you were in love with him. Instead...I don't know, the words said 'I'm in love,' but the face said 'I have to go for a root canal.'"

"That bad, huh?"

"Yeah. Let's go eat some chocolate cake and try to figure out why that is."

"Chocolate cake at eleven in the morning?"

"There is no such thing as a wrong time for chocolate cake."

Meagan's expression was so angelic that Charlie couldn't resist poking at her. "Well, unless you're in the pub drinking beer."

"Oh, yuck. You're right. I stand corrected."

"I don't see why it has to get complicated," Charlie said a half hour later as they were seated in the restaurant.

"So that means you've told him that you love him."

"Are you crazy? Of course I haven't told him. I mean, come on, I only just realized it myself for sure this morning."

"When?" Megan paused with her fork half-way to her mouth.

"Pardon?" Charlie looked up at the quick question.

"When did you realize it this morning? Was it, like, a quiet revelation over the cornflakes?"

"No. It was when he worked so hard to make me laugh after I'd fallen asleep and accidentally left him chained to the bed all night."

"Do I want to hear this, really? Hell, yes. Spill it. Every last wickedly salacious detail."

Charlie did, in very broad, general terms that had M.E. shaking her head, a look of longing on her face.

"I've been out of circulation too long, that's for sure. And I've been aiming at the wrong crowd. I can see that now. I've always gone for the buff guys. Maybe I'd better scope out the local library instead. There's something to be said for the brainy ones. Who knew? Must be all those books they read." She picked up her napkin and waved it as if to cool herself. "Now, when are you going to tell him that you're in love with him?"

"I hadn't planned to do it any time soon. We've only really been together for a few weeks. And, actually, only really *together* together for less than that. There's no rush. I don't see why we can't just, you know, be together."

"That's a lot of togethers that aren't together at all, Charlie. What are you afraid of?"

"What makes you think I'm afraid of anything? I'm not afraid of anything. Not exactly." But she was afraid of something, Charlie thought. She just wasn't certain what. She took a bite of her cake, but it went down hard.

"I'll tell you what you're afraid of. Your Lesley is a house-in-the-suburbs-two-point-five-kids-a-station-wagon-and-a-dog kind of guy."

"Oh, no, now there you're wrong." On this point, Charlie was positive. "You are *so* wrong. He's planning on fixing up and then selling his house. I don't think he has marriage, kids, a dog or a station wagon on his mind at the moment."

"Great, then you can tell him you love him and everything will be fine."

"Great."

"There's that dental surgery look again. You know, Charlie, having an S.O. bears no resemblance whatsoever to living with a father and four brothers."

Charlie felt as if her world had just come to a screeching halt. "What are you talking about? I have no issues with the way I grew up." But even as she said the words, she felt a shiver of revelation race down her spine.

"Oh, no? You've always insisted on being called Charlie, not Charlene. You hung out with your brothers and only boys till I came along. You took a summer job and did your best to erase your femininity, not even telling them you *were* a girl for the first month. You've chosen a career that ensures you mostly work with men, on your own. You're right, girlfriend. No issues going on with you."

"Well, hell." Charlie pushed the rest of her cake away. She had lost her appetite, completely. It turned out she was something she never thought she'd be—a woman with *issues*. Not just a female, but a *complicated female*. Now she had to spend hours on introspection. She hated that more than just about anything.

* * * *

"You're kidding." Percy's words were laced with disbelief.

"Not at all. I am totally, completely, head-over-heels-till-death-do-us-part in love with the woman." When Percy only continued to stare at him, Lesley shook his head.

"Your lack of response amazes me. You're the one who was chiding me for letting something I knew was special slip through my fingers." Lesley looked around the sports bar and noted that it wasn't as crowded as usual for a Sunday afternoon. He raised two fingers for the waiter, then took out his wallet.

"There's a difference between developing a special relationship along the road of life and throwing away your freedom for the remainder of your days. What do you know about this woman, really? I mean, you've only been seeing each other for a few weeks." Percy also took out his wallet and threw a ten dollar bill on the table.

"Ha, a few weeks! We met exactly thirty-three days ago. That's more than an entire month. And what I know is that she's the one for me. That's all I need to know."

"She didn't even go to college."

Lesley narrowed his eyes. "Careful."

"I didn't mean that in a derogatory way. I was just thinking of compatibility, here. It's just—hell, she's just got high school, and you hold a doctorate."

"Two, actually."

"There, see."

Lesley waited until the waiter delivered their beer. Then he sat back and prepared to defend his position. "All that means is that I've amassed knowledge in specific fields. It's not an indication of intelligence. Charlie is a very intelligent woman."

"Look, I'm just worried that you're going to get into a situation that you won't be able to get out of."

"That already happened last night."

"What?"

"Never mind. Percy, you're my best friend and you've known me a long time. Have I ever told you that I was in love before?"

Percy took a long sip from his beer, then set the bottle down gently. "No, and that's what's got me worried."

"Well, I'm worried too. The woman is *work*. I have to be careful that I don't move too fast and scare her away. Or mention the L word or the M word. So I'm only speaking the C word at the moment."

"Women aren't afraid of love and marriage, Lesley. That's our thing."

"Yeah? Well, I've got news for you. That sexist stereotype is passé."

"So, then, what's the C word—commitment or cohabitation?"

"Neither. It's Construction. My biggest problem was figuring out how to keep her around long enough for me to completely win her over. But I came up with a plan that is guaranteed fool-proof."

"Uh oh." To Lesley, it seemed as if Percy was gathering his strength. Or perhaps, his patience.

"Lesley, don't you know that no plan is fool-proof for a sufficiently talented fool?"

"Ha ha."

"Okay Einstein, let's order lunch and then you can lay your latest brainstorm on me."

"Well, now, that sounded facetious. First you claim I'm too much of a genius for the woman I love, now you're implying I'm an idiot."

"As the man who has listened patiently to each hare-brained incarnation of this 'master plan' of yours, I have no problem with this paradox," Percy said as he opened a menu.

Lesley mirrored his friend's action, but didn't really glance at the selections offered. He was too intent on convincing Percy that he knew what he was about. "Well, this time, I can absolutely guarantee you that what I've come up with is definitely going to work."

"Does the expression 'famous last words' mean anything to you?"

"Cynic."

"No, I'm not a cynic, I'm a realist."

"You can usually be counted on to come up with some really good advice. And you did. But now I've spent that time you urged me to take to really get to know her. And I have, and this plan really *is* perfect. Before she knows it, Charlie will be reeled in hook, line and sinker. Trust me."

Chapter 16

His plan was unfolding perfectly.

Lesley smiled as he awaited the arrival of the architect. So far, he had been able to keep Charlie close and off balance. It was, he mused, almost as if she expected him to begin to make demands on her the longer they were together. He wasn't certain where she had gotten the idea that he would. He wondered if she had been subjected to pressure because she'd chosen not to attend university and had instead chosen a career doing what she loved.

He knew first hand what it was like to live with the dashed expectations of ambitious parents. His own had made it quite clear that they felt he should aspire to be more in life than just a *librarian*. If it weren't for all those summers with Aunt Edith and her grounding influence in his life, he might have allowed his parents' perceptions of him to become his reality.

The chiming of the doorbell brought Lesley back to the present. A quick glance at the clock showed him that it was exactly seven.

"Hi, I'm Nathan," the lanky blond man said when Lesley opened the door.

"Lesley. Come in." Lesley shook the man's hand and felt his measure being taken at the same time.

"Charlie tells me you're wanting an addition. I'd like to see the house and the yard out back."

"Upstairs first, then?"

"Great. I went to school with her brother, Cam."

"I was wondering how it was you knew each other."

"I've known Charlie since she was a kid. Even though she was always a fierce little thing and independent as all get out, her brothers still watched out for her. Closely."

"Uh huh. Totally understandable, I suppose. Of course, if taken to the extreme, it might turn a girl into a woman who felt she could only follow her own destiny if she was alone."

"Yeah, most likely. As a kid, she was a lot of work."

"That," Lesley confirmed, "hasn't changed. But then, I can be, too. So I'd say we're well matched."

"Charlie seems to think that you're putting this addition on in order to sell the place."

"I know."

"How long do you hope to keep her thinking that?"

"Every day I get with her is a bonus. With luck, I'll have her moved in when she figures it out."

"Good luck with that." Nathan's tone belied his words.

The examination of the house and grounds didn't take long. Nathan seemed to grasp immediately what it was he wanted. The young architect promised plans within a week.

Once alone again, he went out into the back yard to tend to his Aunt's garden. He had made certain that the man understood these gardens were to remain untouched. He would have to point that out to Charlie as well.

"My, my with all the comings and goings lately, a nosy neighbor is bound to get dizzy!"

Lesley looked up and smiled at Mrs. Crosby.

"You're not a nosy neighbor, Mrs. C. I've just been seeing to some of the things this house needs lately, is all."

"Well, that young woman you've hired sure seems to take her work very seriously. Why, I was almost positive that I saw her truck in your driveway nearly the entire weekend."

"Busted." Lesley beamed up at the woman, then got to his feet, brushing off his hands. "She's a very special woman, Mrs. C."

"Well, I like her. She's very patient with me when I ramble on."
Then the elderly lady looked over the yard and the back of the house.

"My grandson said he thinks that you're fixing up the place to sell
it."

There was such a look of sad resignation on the lady's face that
Lesley had to lean over the fence and plant a kiss on the woman's
cheek.

"No, I'm afraid you're stuck with me living next door to you for a
long, long time to come. Sorry if you were hoping to get new
neighbors. I am having an addition built on, but I'm not planning on
going anywhere. And, if all goes according to plan, I won't be living
here alone, either."

"Oh, why that's marvelous! And would one of those new rooms
you're building on be a nursery?"

The thought of having a child with Charlie momentarily left him
breathless. He felt certain that once she got over her jitters about
getting married, she'd be as eagerly looking forward to having babies
as he was. A little girl who would follow her mom to the construction
site or her dad to the university. A little boy with her wicked smile
and gleaming eyes. Not right away, of course, but when the time was
right. Yeah, that was something to look forward to, all right.

"Well, I am having a couple more bedrooms built on."

"Why, I'm going to go start knitting right away! I just love
making those little sweaters and caps, oh, and they have the most
beautiful wool now for crocheting little baby blankets."

"Mrs. C—" Lesley tried to get her attention, but she was nearly
half way to her back door. He shook his head, a smile tugging at the
corner of his mouth as he realized he hadn't seen her look so excited
in a long time. He'd wait a few days, he mused, as he squatted down
and refocused on the garden. Then he'd go over for tea and fill her in
on what he was working toward.

* * * *

Charlie pretended that her attention was focused on the plate of Virginia ham and scalloped potatoes in front of her and not on her second oldest brother, Cameron. It was a rare occasion in the McKinley household. The last time Charlie and all her brothers had sat around the dining room table, sharing dinner, had been the day before their parents had left on their driving tour. Not only were the senior-most members of the family absent from this evening's proceedings. So, too, was Charlie's sister-in-law, Laura. That little fact told Charlie all she needed to know about the agenda for this evening's dinner conversation. Obviously, Cam's wife wasn't on the same page as he was. From the smirks she could see on the faces of Chad and Clarence, they weren't particularly either. Echoing Cam's one-word opening salvo was just the first tactic in her arsenal. She continued eating for another moment as if eating was the only thing she was capable of doing in the world, and she was doing it in a closet all by herself. Finally, she looked at Chad, who seemed as if he was going to burst out laughing any moment. She winked at him and said, "Pass the milk, please."

When she had finished filling her glass, she sat back and stared at Cam point blank.

"Look, I know why you're here and what you're going to say."

"Well, good. So then—"

"Cameron, I'm sorry if things between you and Laura aren't working out. I really am. But if we're having a family meeting and a vote, then I have to say no, you may *not* move back in here. Absolutely not. I want you to go home, young man, and work out your differences with your wife."

Cam shook his head. "Very funny, baby sister. You know damn well that's not why we're here."

"I don't know about the rest of you, but *I'm* here for the food. Been a while since anyone offered to make such a nice dinner for us." Clarence smiled as if he'd stated the obvious.

"Hey, I'd cook for you heathens once in a while if you'd all pitch in and buy food I could make something with," Chad responded in defense.

"I'm just here because there was free food and big brother Cam told me to be."

"And, Carl, because you sense entertainment in the air and want to suck it up with the rest of us," Clarence said.

"Well, yeah, that too."

"Guys...." Cameron's frown conveyed his unhappiness with this brazen break in ranks.

"Sorry to disillusion you, but I'm not clairvoyant. If you and Laura are doing okay, then I really don't know why you're here—and without her, at that. Because you moving in here would be my business. How I live my life, however, certainly isn't yours."

"Of course you're my business. In Dad's absence, one of us has to step in and keep an eye on you. What do any of us know about this guy you're seeing? None of us have met him. What's wrong with him that you won't bring him around? Listen, kid, you might think you know how to handle your own life, but the very fact that you seem to have trouble forging lasting relationships is a sure sign that you need our guidance."

Well, shit, M.E. had hit the nail on the head. Why had Charlie never noticed what a pain in the ass her brother Cam could be? Though to be honest, were it not for Chad's ill-fated relationship of late, and his resulting tempered heart, he'd have been stern-looking and nodding his head too. Hell, they were going to have a fight. Charlie *hated* fighting with any of her brothers.

"Well, fuck that sideways! The reason I haven't 'forged any relationships,' as you so baldly put it, is because you clowns have turned me right off men."

"Hell, Charlie, if you can't—" Cam surged to his feet.

Charlie pushed her chair back as she rose, tossing her napkin on the table. "I didn't even lose my virginity until I was twenty-five, and then I picked a guy who wanted to do nothing but party and have fun. The next one was no better. He was too busy fawning over himself to pay me much more mind than the attention necessary to ensure he got laid."

"That's all the more reason—" Cam moved away from the table, taking a step toward Charlie.

"For you to butt out of my life! I don't understand this, Cam. I've seen you with Laura. You don't act like a sexist dictator pig where she's concerned. I've listened as you've discussed things; I've seen you treat her like an equal. Don't I at least deserve the same consideration from you that she gets?" At this point they were standing toe-to-toe, voices raised to screaming level.

"I don't have to worry about Laura. She's a mature woman with a degree in finance who's intelligent and capable enough to run her own life!"

Charlie stepped back as if she'd been slapped. A shock wave of silence echoed through the dining room.

"Aw, shit, Cam." Chad had taken his eyes off his sister and narrowed them on his brother.

"You...you think I'm stupid and incompetent, because I don't have letters after my name? That I can't even run my own life because I work with my hands for a living?"

Cameron opened his mouth and then snapped it shut again. Charlie didn't see that his expression was troubled. She couldn't see anything except the huge insult she'd just been dished by her own brother.

Charlie had to get out of there before she did something she avoided at all costs. She swallowed back the tears that threatened. Her anger and pain pulled words meant to slice. "You're worse than a sexist dictator pig. You're a pompous asshole!"

She heard her brothers calling her name, but she didn't want to talk to any of them right now. There was, in fact, only one person she wanted to talk to, to be with. Only one person who could make the hurt go away.

Chapter 17

Tires screeched on pavement. Lesley looked up from the book he was reading, puzzled. Before he could do more than get to his feet, the front door opened and then slammed shut.

"Sorry."

He set his book on the coffee table and walked out to the entrance hallway. Charlie was standing there, her head down, breathing hard.

"Charlie?"

"Sorry I slammed the door."

There was a hitch in her voice, and Lesley's heart melted. He went over to her, set his hands on her shoulders and gently rubbed her arms.

"Sweetheart, what's wrong?"

"Had a fight with my brother."

"Which one?"

"The pompous asshole one."

Oh good. There's only one of those. "I see. Do you want to talk about it, or do you want me to hold you on my lap while you let go and have that cry you're trying so hard not to have?"

"I *hate* crying."

"Me, too. One of the messier aspects of life."

"You cry?"

She looked up at him then and there was such an expression of sorrow on her face, it nearly broke his heart. He took her hand and gently led her into the living room. He was trying not to feel too happy or excited about the fact that she'd come to him. She was upset and hurting, and she'd come to *him*. That was a huge step.

"Sure. My nose gets all red, I have to blow it a gazillion times, my eyes itch and I get these little hiccup-y things afterwards." By this time he'd led her over to the rocker and gently pulled her down onto his lap. Wrapping his arms around her, he said, "Holding back crying can be just as dangerous to your health and well-being as trying to hold in a sneeze. Okay, I'm ready anytime you are. Let 'er rip."

Instead of crying, Charlie laughed softly and relaxed into Lesley's embrace. "Megan said on Sunday that the reason I have issues with commitment, and certain aspects of being female, has to do with my brothers. As close as we've been, she never said anything like that to me before."

"Likely because you didn't need to hear it before."

"I note that you're not surprised."

"That you have issues? Or that your best friend never said anything until now?"

"Either. Both."

"I'm not."

"Oh. Can I ask you a question?"

"Charlie, you can ask me anything in the world."

"Do you think I'm stupid and incompetent because I didn't go to university or college?"

"Absolutely not! Charlie, you're one of the brightest, most perceptive women I've ever met. Incompetent? Lady, you know how to do a hell of a lot more things than I do—and you do them very well."

"Doesn't take any brains to hammer a nail."

"I can't hammer a nail, and just the idea of operating a motorized saw of any kind gives me the heebie-jeebies. Do you think that makes me less than a whole man?"

Her head snapped up at that. "God, no! Of course not."

"What *would* be stupid, Charlie, would be to spend your life doing something you hated because others thought it was what you *should* do. Or to turn your back on the natural talents and gifts you'd been blessed with."

"You really mean that, don't you?"

"Of course I do. And if one of your brothers suggested that for even one moment, then you're right. He is a pompous asshole."

"I've been afraid of what's been happening between us, because I am afraid of commitment."

"I know."

"And part of the reason for that is this sense that I'd have to be 'handled' in a relationship. And tonight is almost a case in point. My brother pisses me off and hurts my feelings, and what do I do? Do I punch him in the face? No, I come running over here to cry on your shoulder."

"I'd like to point out that you've yet to cry."

"Metaphorically."

"Coming to me when you're hurt isn't a sign of weakness, Charlie. It's a sign that you know that with me, you're safe. You can lick your wounds, let your guard down and know that I'm on your side one hundred percent. If something happened to shake me, to hurt me or piss me off, you're the only person *I'd* want to be with. And if I needed back-up, you're the one I'd want in my corner."

"Really?"

"Yeah, really. That's what love is, Charlie. In case I've forgotten to mention it, I love you."

"I love you too, and it's been messing with my head."

For a long moment they simply stared at each other. Lesley could see that Charlie hadn't planned on saying that. "Thank you for giving me the words, sweetheart," he whispered, placing a gentle kiss on her forehead.

"You're welcome."

Lesley snickered. "So, you want I should go over and beat the crap out of your brother for you?"

Charlie laughed out loud. "I don't know. No one's ever offered to do that for me before. I guess I never thought I was the kind of woman that anyone would offer to slay dragons for."

"Well, I'm offering, Charlie. I know you're more than capable of slaying your own dragons and fighting your own battles. But anytime you need me, I'm here."

"I know. Thanks. But, no, I guess I won't have you beat him up. This time. Pompous asshole or not, he's still my brother. Besides, he has a wife who, for reasons that I cannot imagine at the moment, is very fond of him."

"Do you know what I'd like us to do right now?"

"I have an idea."

Lesley smiled. "Besides that. I'd like to just sit here for a while and hold you. That's loving you, too. And maybe you'll begin to see that it doesn't have to hurt or mess with your head at all."

* * * *

After a long, quiet time, Lesley kissed her hair. "Would you like a nice hot bath?"

Charlie felt her insides heat at the thought of sharing a tub of steamy water with him. Lesley was nothing if not inventive when it came to sensual games.

Except he didn't get in with her. He prepared the bath carefully, adding some jasmine scented crystals. Undressing her tenderly, he held her hand while she got into the tub.

"You relax, and I'll bring you something to drink."

She'd been expecting wine, and got hot chocolate. He gave her the mug, lit a couple of candles, put on soft music, and then left her alone for a while.

Lying back in the tub, eyes closed, she relaxed completely. She hadn't actually planned to come to Lesley. There had been no thinking involved at all. In the past, whenever she'd felt the need to escape her brothers, she'd gone to Megan's. That hadn't even occurred to her tonight. She shivered then, as she recalled the words she'd given him—something else that had happened without thought or plan.

Those three words hadn't hurt as much as she thought they would.

When Lesley returned, it was with towels that he'd warmed in the dryer and one of his white tee shirts. He dried her, dressed her, and led her upstairs to his bed.

It wasn't very late, just nine o'clock, but he put her in his bed. Stripping in record time, he crawled naked under the blankets with her, and immediately peeled the shirt from her.

"I know how to be relentless, too." Suiting actions to words, he proceeded to show her.

With hands and lips and tongue, he cherished her. No part of her was left unloved. He suckled her nipples until she mewed and flexed her hips. Then he turned his ministrations to another part of her body. He licked her shoulder, stroked her belly, and caressed her thighs. She had never felt so overwhelmed with sensation. When she was sobbing his name, he took a moment to protect her, then covered her and began a slow, steady penetration.

"I love how you feel inside me," she whispered. Warmth and arousal wound together within her, melting her bones and heating her blood. Everything he did to her felt like heaven. She was content to follow his gentle rhythm, to thrust her pelvis so that she captured his penis deep within her vaginal canal. Flexing her muscles, she squeezed him, making him groan, too.

"God, woman, you have wonderful muscle tone," he rasped. His mouth captured hers in a kiss that was carnal and tender at the same time.

"Your muscle is in pretty good shape, too. Ah, yes. *Just like that.*"

"Come for me, baby. I want to feel you come for me—on me."

"Lesley!" Charlie cried out his name as her orgasm swept through her. Her reaching up and wrapping herself around him was instinctive. Her climax surged higher as she felt his seed spilling hot inside her.

Emotional upheaval, a luxurious bath, and wonderful lovemaking had Charlie's eyes closing in exhaustion. Her last impressions were of Lesley gently pulling her into the haven of his arms, stroking her back and kissing her forehead. "I love you, Charlie," he whispered, and the gentle declaration followed her into sleep.

* * * *

Having left the house the night before without even her purse, Charlie trekked home early to change into her work clothes and then return to Lesley's. A soft smile lit her face as she thought of how sweet he'd been to her. She had never known how good it could be to have a man care for her in such exquisite detail. A part of her wondered if she wasn't being completely…well, *female* about things lately. And a part of her knew, beyond a shadow of a doubt, that she'd go out of her way to do kind and loving things for him if and when he ever needed them.

Could that be it, then? An equal balance of giving and taking, each person in a relationship having turns at being cared for and being caretaker? Well, what the hell was so scary about that?

The house was still quiet when she let herself in. Passing the living room, an unusual sight caught her eye. There, half on the sofa and slipping fast, covered with an afghan, Cam lay snoring.

She *hated* fighting with any of her brothers. She should just chalk up what happened last night to overprotective big brother weirdness, and go about her business.

Like hell she would.

Stomping into the living room, she yanked the covering off him. Having been wrapped around his body, the unfurling of the blanket dumped him onto the floor.

"Shit!"

"Wake up, you worm! I've got a few things to say to you!"

"Argh—what—"

"I said get up!" To underscore her demand, she lightly kicked his legs.

"Crap, come on, Charlie, give me a break! Shit, I haven't even had my coffee yet!"

"Shit and crap? Pretty limited use of vocabulary for a *university graduate*."

"Ugh."

"Another verbal gem!"

"Look, before you tear a strip off my ass, can we at least have coffee?"

"Yeah, if you make it. I have to change for work. Make it snappy, bro, I'll be down in ten minutes."

"Honest to God, Charlene," Cam began as soon as she entered the kitchen a few minutes later. "I have *no* idea where the hell that came from last night."

"I've always believed that things said in the heat of the moment have more than a grain of truth in them. And I find, Cameron, that I'm very disappointed to know that you're such a narrow-minded individual as to hold my lack of formal education against me." Charlie sat down at the table and kept her attention on him.

"You, our brothers and my wife." He looked up and gave her a sheepish smile. "Laura said I couldn't come home until I apologized to you."

"Waiting here."

"Yeah, yeah, I'm getting to it. Damn, you haven't changed. You still don't know how to accept an apology gracefully."

She kept her eyes on him as he got up and poured coffee for them both. Once he sat again she shook her head. "And you still don't know how to give one. It's a comfort, isn't it, to revisit our childhood this way?"

"Like hell."

"Yeah, my thought, too. And you're stalling."

"Charlie, I'm sorry I said what I did. I'm sorry that I implied you were stupid and incompetent. You're neither. I spent a lot of time last night thinking about what I said. I guess I was really disappointed when you didn't go to college or university. Especially considering that you're the smartest of us all."

This was too much like past conversations for her to just let it go. She set her mug on the table and knew her tone was sarcastic when she said, "And I'm disappointed that you didn't go into landscaping. We could have built some beautiful homes together, brother mine."

"I *hate* gardening."

"I know." She knew the frost in her tone stopped the conversation cold.

"Okay, I get your point," Cam said quietly after a bit. "And I've always known and believed that we each have to follow the path that's right for us. I guess I just need to get that from my head to my heart."

"Mmm, yes. And quickly, before you have children of your own."

"Good point."

They offered each other tentative smiles.

"So, am I forgiven?"

"I guess." But her grin took the sting out of the reluctance.

"I still want to meet the guy. That hasn't changed."

"I figured. You'll meet him. Sooner or later. I'm still trying to get used to the idea that I'm in love with the man. But the more I think about it, the less scary it becomes." She was a little surprised that he put his hand on hers. They weren't, for the most part, a touchy-feely family.

"Being in love isn't scary, honey. Laura's the best thing that ever happened to me, and I can't for one moment envision my life, now, without her in it."

"But she wouldn't let you come home till you apologized to me."

"Yeah. And that was the right thing for me to do. Your life partner is on your side, always. Sometimes that means gently pointing out when you've goofed, as I did last night. If it's any comfort to you, I'll do the same thing. Just as soon as the woman makes a mistake."

Charlie couldn't stop her chuckle. "You might have a long wait there, Cameron."

"Don't I know it," he agreed, a huge smile accompanying that statement.

"Go home to your wife before I change my mind and beat you up."

"A PhD, huh?"

"He has two, actually."

"Maybe next to him, *I'll* feel stupid and incompetent."

"We can only hope."

Chapter 18

On days like this, Lesley envied Charlie. June had arrived in all her glory, doing her best to imitate summer. Today in particular the sky was a mesmerizing blue, the sun warm, and the breeze just light enough to tickle the senses with the fragrance of life.

Working outside, Charlie might occasionally get a whiff of manure, but at least she didn't have to share table space with it.

It was probably not a real good idea to think that way about attending special meetings with the head of the University, who also happens to be my boss. The meeting had taken the better part of the day.

It seemed lately that Lesley's little imp was, for the most part, silent. The odd word here or there, like now. *He's probably in a perpetual state of sexual exhaustion.* Lesley smiled. With any luck, his imp would stay that way for a long time to come.

He turned his attention back to his laptop, which sat on the keyboard tray of his desk. After keying in a search request, he opened it flat, pushed the tray in, and turned his attention to his office PC. He wanted to finish going through the list of books about to be removed from the stacks and stored. It was a job he should have assigned to a student, but he was just anal enough to want to check it himself, just in case. Another hour of this and then he'd be homeward bound. Home to Charlie.

She didn't stay with him every night, but it was close. There were a few things of hers hanging in his closet, and he had very quietly cleaned out a couple of drawers for her to use. Her toothbrush touched bristles with his all day.

He had begun to include her in other ways too. It had only taken Nathan a short time to deliver preliminary plans for the addition. Lesley had needed Charlie to explain just what the heck he was looking at, as he couldn't make any sense out of the drawings. He also elicited her opinion on various aspects of the project, and when she would try to say, "Well, this is your house, Lesley," he'd say, "Yeah, but I was just curious. What would you do if it was yours?" The result was that he was beginning to see the kind of things she'd like, and had instructed Nathan to incorporate them into the design.

Today she had told him that the concrete for the basement was set, and she'd install the footings and begin to build the deck. From there, as best as he could understand, it would be walls, the second story deck and then the roof.

In the mean time, he was doing all he could to ensure that their relationship had as solid a foundation as the addition to his house did.

* * * *

Charlie stood back, her hands on her hips, and stretched her spine. The deck was perfect, straight and even and very well made if she did say so herself. Taking her gloves off, she checked her watch and saw that it was nearly three-thirty.

Tom came around from the front of the house, having deposited the debris he'd gathered into the industrial sized bin sitting in the driveway.

"It's looking good, Charlie. I think I like working on this addition better than anything we've done. It's like we're making something new here."

"We *are* making something new here."

"I have to leave now if I'm going to keep that dentist appointment. But hey, if you need—"

"You're not going to use me to get out of that one, Tom. Go ahead. I can carry on without you. If you're not coming in tomorrow, give me a call on my cell, okay?"

"You got it."

Alone, Charlie reached for her thermos. She'd filled it with cold water to reduce the trips indoors during the day. Of course, she didn't bother to pack a lunch anymore. Lesley was always leaving things in the fridge for her—either leftovers from their dinner of the night before or, on the rare days when she hadn't stayed over, there was something made just for her on one of the shelves.

"Well, I was certainly worried, let me tell you."

"I beg your—"

Resigned to a Mrs. C. conversation, Charlie had spun around, a ready smile on her face. She grinned when she saw the elderly lady seated at the patio table in her back yard, facing away, with a portable phone held to her ear.

Deciding to just sit and take a bit of a break, Charlie sat down in one of the Adirondacks near the garden. Leaning back, she closed her eyes. The sun was warm, she could smell the lily of the valley blooming, and the song of birds lulled her into a place of relaxation. Mrs. C's words danced at the edge of her consciousness.

"Oh, I know. It would have been like losing her all over again. As you know, we were neighbors for nearly fifty years. Why, I remember the very first day that dear, sweet boy came to stay for the summer. A more serious and stifled child you never saw. Let me tell you, Edith certainly had her work cut out for her. Why, do you know his parents didn't even let him bring any toys? Edith and I were both aghast at that, even more so when we found out the poor little mite didn't even have any."

Charlie and Lesley had talked a few times about his parents, and how he was raised, and each time she'd sensed that he was being kinder in retrospect than was warranted. She tried to imagine being eight and not having any toys, having to devote every minute of her day to chasing a goal her parents had set for her. She couldn't imagine it, and marveled at the well-rounded, well-adjusted man Lesley had become.

"Well, yes, but as I told you—oh, I didn't? Well, I don't know where my mind is these days! I found out he's not moving away after all, you see? Isn't that wonderful! It made me so, so happy when he told me that. No, he's fixing up the house to live in. Oh, and it gets better. You'll never guess!"

Charlie frowned. Mrs. C. was still talking about Lesley. She tried to search her memory, certain the other woman was wrong. But then she realized, he'd never *said* he was selling the house. And now that she thought about it, selling it didn't make sense on a personal level. He told her he'd had the best times of his life here. He even asked her to be especially careful of his Aunt Edith's garden. No, selling it didn't make any sense at all.

"All right, I'll give you a huge clue. One of those new rooms he's adding on is a nursery."

He wanted to start a gardening business? Charlie sat up in her chair and shook her head. Obviously, she'd dozed off and was listening to a dream-altered conversation. It was time to get back to work.

"I am not kidding, I heard it from his own lips. That nice Dr. Farmer is going to be a daddy. Of course he's getting married. Well, what would you expect? To a nice professional woman, like himself, of course. I've been knitting up a storm, let me tell you. Edith would be so happy. Hold on, Mildred, while I go into the house. I want to make a cup of tea."

Charlie sat frozen in her chair, unable to move. Lesley...going to be a *father*? Getting married? She shook her head slowly, trying to deny what she'd just overheard with her own two ears. That couldn't be right. And yet...hadn't a part of her known all along that the man was just too good to be true? Maybe...maybe the reason she had been having such a hard time accepting the idea of commitment was that her subconscious knew it was a lie all along.

It had all been a lie, one he had fabricated just so he could get her to work on his house. It all made sense, now. She recalled the times her brothers had conned her into doing one thing or another for them, using male puppy-dog smiles and lies. Carl, complaining that he didn't feel well and asking her to do his grade eleven science project, just so he could go off smooching with Mary Ellen Crombie, that slut. Cam and Chad had each tricked her into doing their laundry and cleaning their rooms in the past. Though nothing that had gone before prepared her for this latest male betrayal.

Charlie felt a sharp burning in her chest as she understood, finally, what Lesley had done, what he meant to do. He was engaged to some bimbo with a degree and they were going to raise little doctoral candidates in the house that Charlie helped to build? They were going to be making love and cooing noises in the bedroom she was constructing with her sweat and heart and strength?

What was she, a convenient side piece, an easy lay with the added benefit of cut-rate labor?

Charlie felt her temper spike, eclipsing the pain. That bastard! That miserable, two-faced, piled higher and deeper bastard! Did he think that she was just some brainless floozy who would meekly go away on the eve of his damn wedding to his damn *professional woman* fiancé?

When she got her hands on him she'd…she'd…do something.

Jumping to her feet, she charged into the house. That prick would be at work behind his snooty desk in that snooty library on campus. Running upstairs, she grabbed one item from the bedroom. Racing down the stairs she stopped long enough to root through her toolbox for another. On her way out the door she scooped a couple more from his office.

He and his pregnant poopsie were probably laughing at her behind her back this very minute! She narrowed her eyes, pain warring with anger. Using every bit of her will, she made sure that anger won. By the time she was through with Lesley Farmer, the laugh would definitely be on him!

* * * *

At the sound of the door opening, Lesley's head snapped up, words of dismissal on his lips. He smiled as soon as he saw Charlie.

"Sweetheart, this is a nice surprise. Just let me save this file."

She said nothing, just stalked over to him. He'd no sooner taken his fingers off his keyboard than she swung his chair around so that he was facing her.

"Charlie—" He was silenced by her lips, hot, bruising hot on his. He lost himself in the kiss, dimly aware of his surroundings. His laptop had just beeped to announce a completed task, and then cold steel snapped around his wrist.

"Charlie, what are you doing?" His eyes were on his left wrist manacled to the chair, and he didn't see the tape coming.

"This is called pay back, you two-timing, slimy bastard."

Surprise at having tape pressed roughly against his mouth and confusion from the words Charlie hurled froze him in place for just a moment. Then he began to struggle, but that was futile. So was talking.

"Mrmph!"

"Screwing me while you've got a fiancé, a *pregnant* fiancé, waiting in the wings!"

Lesley shook his head, trying to deny the ridiculous accusation. His words, of course, were unintelligible. He would have thought Charlie was just pulling his leg, but for the very real tears that were streaming down her face.

"Don't try to deny it! I overheard Mrs. Crosby telling someone all about it. Engaged to a professional woman, she says. Building a nursery, she says. Well *I* say, fuck you!"

By now Lesley's right hand was taped to his chair with a very strong gray tape. Looking down, he imagined she had slapped the same stuff over his mouth. As her words penetrated, he tried to figure out just how in hell...*oh, shit.* As if it had just happened, he could envision chatting with Mrs. C. over the back fence the day the architect had been there. The lady's happy grin seemed to mock him in memory, as did the words about making sweaters and caps and little blankets. He had meant to go over and straighten her out, but had totally forgotten.

He jerked when Charlie ripped open his shirt, sending the buttons flying. Then, as he saw her next weapon, he began to shake his head, vigorously, in denial.

"The two of you laughing at me behind my back. Well, you and your little bitch can just laugh about this!"

Chapter 19

For a long moment, no one said a word.

Percy and Melissa were struck dumb. Lesley was doing his best to get them to move, to come over and help him. He thought he was being rather obvious, considering that he was gagged and restrained and bouncing around like a jumping bean. But he could see where their attention was. He really couldn't blame them for being transfixed. He'd spent several minutes staring at it himself.

Their eyes were on the colorful artwork on Lesley's bared chest and abdomen. He knew Mr. Evil Scowling Face glared back at them, every much as menacing looking in black and red magic marker as he imagined he was himself.

Melissa shook her head and took a step forward. Percy placed a hand on her arm, forestalling her.

"Melissa…may I call you Melissa?"

"Um…sure."

"Melissa, do you have a best friend?"

"Ah…sure…sir? Dr. Farmer—"

"Lesley will keep for just a moment."

Lesley didn't share this sentiment. He let them know in the only way he could—with a garbled noise—that he wanted his freedom *now*.

"Melissa, if your best friend ever utters the words, 'this is the perfect plan, trust me,' I want you to bring this moment to mind."

"I will," Melissa finally replied when Percy raised his eyebrow after waiting for several moments. "May I *please* go help Dr. Farmer now?"

"Be my guest."

The young woman hurried around the desk and, starting with the tape covering his mouth, began to peel it back. Both rescuer and rescued winced as it came off with difficulty.

"Melissa."

She looked up when Percy called her name.

"Say cheese." He used his cell phone for the snapshot.

"Thanks for that." Lesley's voice had a bite to it. "Now my embarrassment is complete. Could you at least shut the damn door?"

Chuckling, Percy complied. Then he walked over to his friend and showed him the picture he'd just taken.

"A good likeness. Both mugs."

"You're a funny man, Percy. Shit!" He nearly bellowed that last as Melissa, trying to peel the tape off his arm, inadvertently ripped out some hair. "Sorry," he apologized when she'd jumped back away from him. "I'm sorry, Melissa. I didn't mean to yell at you."

"That's okay, Dr. Farmer. I think I'd be yelling, too."

"Oh, hell, call me Lesley. Formality under these circumstances is rather ridiculous."

"Okay, Lesley. Ah...I could go downstairs to the gift shop and get you a sweatshirt to wear, since your shirt seems to be ruined."

"Thank you, Melissa. That would be great."

By the time the young woman retuned with the garment, Percy had just managed to jimmy open the handcuffs. Lesley rubbed his wrist where he'd made it raw from tugging against the unrelenting steel.

"Well, friend, other than a little inconvenience and embarrassment, you're not faring too badly. If the lady had been really pissed at you, she could have brought her nail gun or her chainsaw."

"Oh, she was pissed, all right. And how did you know Charlie did this?"

"Because it's such a girl thing," Melissa answered, then cringed. "Sorry. I shouldn't be making light of...do you want me to call Campus security? Or the police?"

"Good God, no! In a convoluted way, I deserved this."

"I can't believe you'd ever do anything to deserve this."

Percy patted Melissa's shoulder. "Believe it." To Lesley he said, "For a man who's just been bound, gagged, and decorated, you seem pretty chipper."

"She was mad, and she was crying because she got it in her head that I was cheating on her."

"And that makes you happy?" Melissa asked, her confusion obvious.

"What makes him happy is that the lady wouldn't have been either of those two things if she didn't love him ridiculously."

"Ah. You know, I think I'll just call it a day."

"Go ahead. Oh, and Melissa?"

The young woman turned and gave her boss a smile. "I won't tell a soul. I promise."

"Thanks."

Percy waited until they were completely alone.

"So, what's your next step, Einstein?"

"Tracking Charlie down." Lesley turned off both of his computers, and then rubbed his face with his hands. "You know, there actually is a regressive part of me that wants to turn the little minx over my knee and paddle her ass."

"I think I can understand that."

"Mostly, though, I just want to find her and set her straight. What she did to me was nasty, but she was hurting, Percy. And I hate that something I did —or, rather, didn't do— was the cause of that."

"Oh, man, you are sloppy in love. I have to meet this woman."

"Hopefully, you'll get that chance."

* * * *

"He...he...he was...was so sweet, you know? When...when he...put his mind to it he was *sooo* sweet. And I love him, the bastard."

Megan Elizabeth poured more wine into Charlie's glass, and handed her another bunch of tissues. "Charlie, please tell me what happened? Why is Lesley a bastard?"

"She's p...pregnant."

"Who's pregnant?"

"I don't know! Some...some b..bimbo with a PhD."

"Charlie, bimbos don't have PhDs. They can't even *spell* PhD. Who told you this unnamed bimbo was pregnant, or that it was Lesley's child?"

"She's been knitting up a storm."

"The pregnant bimbo?"

"Noooo....Mrs. C."

Megan patted Charlie's back, murmured "there, there," and waited for this latest round of weeping to subside.

"Charlie, tell me what happened. From the beginning!"

Straightening up, and with a lot of sputtering at first, Charlie related the events of the late afternoon. She tried not to cry, but the tears didn't seem to want to stop. She repeated, word for word, as best as she could recall, the conversation she'd overheard. She also, with head bowed, told her best friend what she'd done to Lesley in revenge.

"First, this was a conversation you overheard. And you overheard only one half of a conversation, at that."

"Well," Charlie hiccupped, and rubbed her reddening nose with a tissue, "the words were rather damning." Her eyes were itching, and in sympathy, M.E. got up, went to the bathroom, and came back with a cool, damp face cloth. They took a time out while Charlie laid the cloth on her closed eyelids. The entire time she was shuddering and sobbing, but trying to get control of herself. After several minutes, she removed the cloth and returned her attention to her friend.

"Second," M.E. continued, giving Charlie a searing glare, "this half conversation was being spoken by Mrs. C., the lady you described as being your Great Aunt Katie's cosmic twin. The same Great Aunt Katie, I will remind you, who thinks 'moron' is a nationality, and that the way to make pickled beets is to soak them in whiskey."

"Ah—"

"But of course, when you asked Lesley about this, he *must* have confirmed it all."

"Well…I didn't exactly give him the chance to…ahem…say anything."

"No, really? Why, Charlie McKinley, you didn't just assume the worst and conduct a pre-emptive strike, did you?"

"Hey, you're supposed to be my best friend!"

"I am. Which is why I am going to get you drunk and put you to bed. Right after I point out the obvious. The man you've been falling in love with, the man you've been describing to me over the past several weeks doesn't sound like the kind of man who would connive and sneak around, the way he would have had to do for this to be true. Is he that kind of man, Charlie? Really?"

Charlie looked into Megan's eyes and knew the truth. Of course Lesley wasn't that sort of man. Unfortunately that realization, coupled with the vivid memory of what she'd done to him just that afternoon, brought fresh tears that flowed faster and harder.

"Noooo…." Her wail was long and pitiful, and she put her head down on the table, the perfect picture of complete misery.

"There, there. Drink up, pass out. And when you wake up we'll see what we can do to fix this."

"I'll never be able to fix it! He hates me now. I know he does! *I* hate me now. Oh, God, what have I done? My one and only chance at happiness, and I ruined it!"

* * * *

After the third blistering pounding of the door, it opened.

"Where is she?" Lesley stormed past the man he'd seen at the basketball game and the dance club.

"She's not here."

He had suspected that, since Charlie's truck was missing.

"Where is she?"

"You don't mind if I ask why you want to know?"

"Are you the pompous asshole?"

"No, that would be my brother, Cam, but he's reformed. I'm Chad."

"Look…your sister is, or I should say *was* upset. I need to see her, as soon as possible."

Charlie's home was his third stop. He had gone home first, and spied Charlie's tools where she'd left them. He'd wasted precious time gathering and securing them inside the house. He knew they were important to her, and she'd be sick if they were damaged or stolen. Next, he had gone over to Mrs. Crosby's and corrected the impression he'd left her with a couple of weeks before. He had smiled when she said, "Well of course, I knew you'd be marrying Charlie. I just thought she was…er…expecting."

He didn't, of course, tell that sweet little old lady what had happened earlier that day. He just left as soon as was politely possible and headed over to the McKinley residence.

It was nearing seven in the evening, and Lesley was worried sick. He didn't think Charlie would do anything foolish or bring harm to herself in any way, but he couldn't get the image of her tears out of his mind.

"What the hell did you do to her?" Chad demanded. A shove accompanied the angry question. Lesley could immediately see where Charlie got her attitude.

"What did I do to her? What did *I* do? I didn't do a damn thing. Your sister, on the other hand, marched into my office, handcuffed one arm to my chair, duct taped the other one, gagged me, and then did this!" He pulled up his shirt, not caring if her brother laughed or not. He just wanted to find Charlie and knew he needed this man's help to do it.

Chad didn't laugh. Instead, he asked quietly, "Where'd she get the handcuffs?"

Oh hell. "You had to pick that."

"Yeah, it just kind of jumped out at me."

Lesley dropped his shirt and eyed the man before him. Standing with his arms folded across his chest, his legs apart, it was clear that this interview wasn't going to go well for him unless he could gain some sympathy.

"Where she got the handcuffs is irrelevant. How she got both my arms pinned before I realized what was happening is also not a matter for your concern. However, since you are, in all likelihood, going to be one of my brothers-in-law, I will tell you that in an indirect way what happened was my fault. Charlie was given a false impression with regard to the work she's been doing—"

"You mean the wild hare you sold her about fixing your place up for resale, when all the time you were just trying to keep her hanging around? We already figured that one out for ourselves," a younger man said as he came into the room. "So, what's up?"

Before Lesley could speak, Chad answered.

"She bellied him."

"Oh, man," said the younger brother, his expression sympathetic, as he covered his belly with both arms. "It took me weeks to get the marker off. Worst of all, I had to take gym class at high school and everyone in the change room saw it." He turned his attention back to

Lesley. His voice was serious when he said, "You'll think twice before dozing off next time, when she's pissed."

"He wasn't asleep," his brother informed him. "She stalked to his office, handcuffed one arm to his chair, used duct tape to secure the other one, gagged him, and bingo."

"Where'd she get the handcuffs?"

"That's where you came in."

The younger man introduced himself as Clarence then aligned himself with his brother. Lesley exhaled deeply, arms akimbo, eyes on his shoes. Perhaps the brothers thought he was feeling defeated. In truth, he was counting to ten, twice. Once for each of them.

When he looked up, he had his temper under control but was no less serious, no less determined than when he had come in. "Where, do you imagine, will I find Charlie?"

"Probably at Megan's place."

A third brother joined them, and Chad, using his thumb to point behind him, said, "That's the pompous asshole."

"Cam, I'm not sure you should tell him where she is. Wait till you hear—"

Cam smiled. "I already did. Megan lives over on Crescent Ave. The house number is fifteen twenty-one, and her apartment's at the top of the stairs on the right side of the house."

Lesley nodded. "So where's the other one?"

"Carl has a gig tonight, playing at the Screaming Mimi."

"Can't say as I've ever visited the place," Lesley said, considering.

"Younger crowd, too many fights," Cam acknowledged. Then, "You going to marry our sister?"

"If she'll have me. First I have to find her and get her to listen to the sweet voice of reason."

Three men looked at each other, and then simultaneously wished him good luck. Lesley wondered if it was luck he was going to need.

Chapter 20

"She looks so sweet and innocent, doesn't she?" Despite the assurance he'd received from Megan that Charlie was down for the count, Lesley kept his voice low.

"You don't sound as if you hate her. You don't even sound all that mad."

"I don't hate her, Megan. I love her. Still working on the mad, though."

"Charlie has always been one to shoot first and ask later. You should know, though, that before she passed out she was crying. She hated herself for what she did."

"You misunderstand me, Megan. I'm not mad at her, but at myself. I've fucked up this entire relationship, royally, right from the beginning."

He looked up when he felt Megan staring at him.

"I don't suppose you have any brothers? A twin would be nice."

Lesley laughed. "No, sorry."

"Oh well. It's only happened a couple of times before, but once Charlie is out, she's out. You could set a bomb off and I doubt it would wake her. You won't likely get a peep out of her till morning. Sorry. I took advantage of her misery and got her drunk on purpose. I thought it was the only way we'd both get any sleep tonight."

Lesley heard a hint of regret in her words, but he only smiled.

"Well, then, I guess she won't wake up while I'm taking her home with me, will she?"

Without a second thought, Lesley lifted Charlie into his arms. "Get the door, will you?"

Megan didn't move for about two seconds. Then she ran ahead, opening the door to the outside, and then trotting down the steps to open the passenger side door of his car. .

"Tell her I'll call her tomorrow."

"Will do. Let her brothers know where she is, all right? I don't want them worrying."

"Okay, if you insist. It's your ass."

Leslie chuckled as he situated Charlie in the front passenger side of his car and managed to get the seat belt around her.

"How do you think I knew where to find her in the first place?"

* * * *

As predicted, Charlie didn't awaken. Not during the fifteen-minute drive across town, nor when he left her alone in the car just long enough to open the front door of his house. He was smiling as he carried her up the stairs to his bed. Efficiently, and without dallying, he stripped her and put her into one of his tee shirts. He really liked the way she looked wearing nothing but one of his shirts. He took a moment to fill a pitcher with ice water and grab the aspirin bottle. He had no idea if she'd wake up with a hangover or not, but once she awoke he wasn't letting her out of his sight until they got things sorted out between them.

Another perfect plan, he thought.

He wanted, very much, to crawl into the bed with her. To gather her into his arms. To hold and caress her, kiss and possess her. But what he felt for her, what he believed they already had together was so much more than the physical. Making love was a big part of their relationship—maybe, right now, the biggest part of it. But it wasn't all, nor would it be the most of it in years to come.

So instead of climbing into the bed and snuggling her, he muscled a chair into the room, grabbed an extra blanket for himself from the linen closet and settled in to watch over her.

He'd been fretting over showing her that a commitment to him didn't have to take anything away from who and what she was. He had used what she was to keep her close, and now as the hours of the night crept by, he knew that tactic hadn't been just a part of a plan. He was, quite frankly, in awe of what she could do. She worked using wood and brick and cement to build something that would bring comfort and joy and last beyond a human lifetime. How special was that?

He managed a facility where others came to learn. He provided a service and a resource for others, and while what he'd chosen as a career satisfied and pleased him, at the end of the day there was no marker left behind, really, to show his passage.

That would only come, for him, in the life and the children he made with the woman he loved.

He settled back into the chair, put his feet on the end of the bed, and closed his eyes. He had always been a light sleeper and would know when Charlie awakened. And he hoped that when she did, he would have the words he'd need to win her.

* * * *

As Charlie began to awaken, she was conscious of several things at once. She was warm and drowsy, with a nasty pounding in her head just waiting for her to open her eyes to pounce. She recalled every moment of the day before as if it had just happened.

She could smell Lesley, and that scent filled her with love and longing. She thought it was a particularly cruel trick for her mind to play on her, but it was no less than she deserved.

In one insane, unreasonable and jealous moment, she had ruined the best thing that had ever happened to her.

She felt movement on the bed. Bless M.E. for having likely stayed home from work to take care of her. At least she still had her best friend.

"What time is it?" Was that raspy, croaky voice hers? *Headache and sore throat. Well-earned souvenirs of a crying jag and drinking binge and generally asinine behavior.*

"Just after ten. How are you feeling?"

Oh, God. Swallowing hard, she opened her eyes. She knew why she'd smelled him. She was in his bed, though how she had come to be here escaped her at the moment. Gathering her courage, she turned her head toward his voice.

There were signs that he'd had a rough night. His morning beard was thick, the clothes he wore looked rumpled, and a blanket lay across his lap. Then the meaning of what she was looking at became clear. *He hates me so much he can't even bring himself to share the bed with me.*

She tried to find her voice. She wanted to tell him that she was fine, and as soon as she got dressed, she would leave him in peace. She thought she might just be able to keep it together long enough to do that.

She had ruined the best thing that had ever happened to her, so stubbornly stupid about being in control and not committing that she'd missed what was so clear to her now. Had she ever thought Lesley Farmer wasn't her type? How shallow and blind of her! A type was more than physical appearance, more than superficial qualities. That's all she'd had before, because deep inside she was determined that no other males were going to push her around or tell her what to do. But a life's mate was not a person who sought to control. In the time she'd spent with Lesley, he'd never tried to tell her what to do, or how to do it. He'd treated her, her time, and her work, with respect. But had she returned the favor? Had she ever really given due consideration to the sheer brilliance of the man? No, she'd not given that a passing thought.

How terribly tragic that she was only just seeing him for the treasure that he was, now, when it was too late. She felt her hold on her emotions begin to slip, and knew it was time to leave. She should ask where her clothes were, get dressed and go.

But the words wouldn't come. She felt the tears form, and accepted that she was going to lose it when her vision blurred and she could barely see him. She hated feeling like an ass, but right now, she'd take that over this deep, wrenching pain that engulfed her.

She blinked, and he seemed to move. Then she knew he was sitting on the side of the bed.

"Let me help you sit up. I've got some aspirins and water right here."

"How can you be nice to me? I'm a horrible, horrible person and I'm so sorry that I screwed everything up!"

She burst into tears, and felt herself gathered close and held tenderly.

"You better watch how you talk about the woman I love."

"How can you still love me? I should be flogged!"

"Flogging is a bit heavy, but hey, if you want to take turns with spanking, I'm game to give it a try."

She almost laughed at that. Instead, she wrapped her arms around him and held on as if she was never going to let go

"I'm sorry. I'm sorry. I was so sure deep inside that you couldn't possibly love me that the first hint of a doubt sent me over the edge. I should have asked. I should have come to you and told you about what I'd overheard Mrs. C. say."

"Oh baby, please stop crying. You're killing me."

"I can't help it. I was such an idiot, and I *hate* being an idiot. And last night, when I realized that I'd fucked up, I was so scared that you'd never want to see me again. I'd hate that even more than being an idiot."

Lesley took her by the shoulders and moved her back just enough so he could wipe her tears and look her in the eyes. "We've both fucked up, Charlie. I don't like being an idiot any more than you do."

"How have you been an idiot?"

"I kept thinking I had to have a plan, or a scheme. I should have simply been honest with you, right from the beginning. There's just something about you, Charlie, something that was simply irresistible, that got to me on every level from the first moment we met. It wasn't just sexual, though that was the most obvious aspect. A man doesn't suddenly change his nature—nor does a woman. It never really made sense that we'd be each other's meaningless affair, when that was so very clearly not who either one of us was. But I couldn't really believe that you could be it for me either, not those first few days. In that, I was as much of a pompous ass as your brother. I thought I knew my type, but *you're* my type, Charlie. You're my mate. If you'll have me."

"Oh God. Oh God, I don't deserve a second chance, but I'm going to take it!"

The time for talking was over. Charlie fastened her lips on his, pouring all the love she felt for him into her kiss. Trembling fingers, male and female, removed clothing, stroked skin, stoked passions. Together they rolled on the condom

"I need you inside me, Lesley. I need to feel your cock pulsing within me."

"Like this," Lesley hissed as he laid her flat and impaled her in one sure thrust.

Charlie wrapped herself around him, all of her muscles working to hold and caress him. "Yes, like this. I'm home now. I'm home."

Their hips moved together quickly, both of them intent on only one thing. There would be time for finesse later. Cuddling and cherishing would come. But right now, they both needed the explosive kind of orgasm they'd each only ever known together.

"Now, now, now," she chanted and held him closer, feeling him come inside her. Her pussy convulsed around him, as if her womb was drinking his seed. "I love you."

"I love you, too, Charlie. You're it for me." He thrust in a slow, measured rhythm. Her gaze locked with his as his penis got harder and filled every inch of her. He smiled when she flexed her hips, using her inner muscles to squeeze him.

"Faster," she urged.

"Make me," he challenged.

She raised her hips and flipped him over, rising above him, riding him deeply. She felt the tip of his cock hit her cervix. The sensation was just on the edge between pleasure and pain, a sensation with an eroticism all its own. She rocked slowly for a long moment, tilting her pelvis to feel him better.

Then he put a finger in his mouth, wet it, and brought it to her clitoris.

She gasped, instantly on the edge. She had thought to torture him with passion, but thinking ceased as her body took over, as she rode him faster and faster.

They came long and hard and together.

As rapture eased, heart rates and breathing calmed, Lesley gathered Charlie into his arms, pulled the blankets around them, and snuggled her close.

"She said she was knitting baby things."

Lesley chuckled. "I know. She thought I was going to sell the place and move away. I had to reassure her that wasn't going to happen. She'd seen your truck in the driveway that first weekend you stayed over, so she knew something was up. So I had to set her straight."

"I still don't understand why she was knitting baby clothes."

"That's simple. I told her I was staying, and hopefully wouldn't be living here alone. She asked me then if one of the rooms we were building was going to be a nursery. All I could think about at that moment was how fantastic it would be if we made a child together, and right then there was nothing more I wanted than to give you my baby. I guess it showed on my face—"

"Now I understand. But...no, never mind."

"No way, Charlie. No more crossed signals. But what?"

"She said you were going to marry a professional woman—professional, like yourself."

"Ah, that's what did it."

"Yeah. Sorry."

He raised himself up on one arm and stroked her face gently. "You're a professional woman, sweetheart. You have a company of your own, a career, and you're every bit as much the professional as I am. We're equals, love, and you'd better start believing that."

"Okay."

He bent down, kissed her, then snuggled her close again.

"You say okay, but you still haven't answered my question."

"Which question?" She was too distracted by the flavor of his neck, right then, to remember whatever question he may have asked.

"Will you have me?"

There was just the smallest note of doubt in his words. Charlie stopped her nibbling long enough to look him square in the eyes.

"Are you kidding? You've got looks, brains, a fantastic body, and a terrific house. And you've got me. Truth is, Lesley Farmer, you're simply irresistible."

"So are you. You and I, Charlie McKinley, were made for each other."

MADE FOR EACH OTHER

THE END

WWW.MORGANASHBURY.COM